DC PIERSON
THE BOY WHO COULDN'T SLEEP AND NEVER HAD TO

DC Pierson was born and raised in Phoenix, Arizona. He graduated from New York University in 2007 with a degree in writing for television. His comedy group DERRICK made a feature film called *Mystery Team*. He publishes short stories and unsolicited opinions on his website, dcpierson.com. This is his first novel.

The Boy Who Couldn't Sleep and Never Had To

The Boy Who Couldn't Sleep and Never Had To

a novel

DC Pierson

VINTAGE BOOKS

A Division of Random House, Inc.

New York

FIRST VINTAGE BOOKS EDITION, FEBRUARY 2010

Copyright © 2010 by DC Pierson

Library of Congress Cataloging-in-Publication Data
Pierson, DC
The boy who couldn't sleep and never had to: a novel /
by DC Pierson.—1st ed.
p. cm.
[1. Friendship—Fiction.   2. High schools—Fiction.   3. Schools—Fiction.
4. Sleep—Fiction.   5. Cartoons and comics—Fiction.   6. Science fiction.]
I. Title. II. Title: The boy who could not sleep and never had to.
PZ7.P6162Boy 2010
[Fic]—dc22   2009021984

Vintage ISBN: 978-0-307-47461-2

Book design by Debbie Glasserman

www.vintagebooks.com

Printed in the United States of America
10   9   8   7   6   5   4

TO TREVOR, MY FIRST BEST FRIEND

The Boy Who Couldn't Sleep and Never Had To

PROLOGUE

All the newspapers and TV pundits are calling this fall's freshman college class the "Symnitol Generation," but if the activity up and down my dorm hallway is any indication, this fall's freshman college class is the "Stand Around Each Other's Laptops and Play The First Thirty Seconds Of Every Song On The Hard Drive Generation." The noise makes it hard to sit and write this but not impossible.

This dorm is called Allerton and it's old and it used to be something else but nobody can agree exactly what. A Catholic girls' school dormitory or a Catholic girls' school school-building or a clothing mill where lots of Catholic girls worked. I am not used to old buildings, and the things that are commonplace to you if you're from the East Coast or anywhere people have inhabited for a while, like radiators or old brass doorknobs covered in several layers of drippy white paint or windows that creak when you open them by turning a knob, are sort of exciting. Everything where I grew up grew up with me. I think the first time I stepped inside a building that was built before 1950, we were out of state on vacation.

Orientation Week they encourage you to keep your doors open to foster a friendly and open atmosphere. A girl whose name I heard several times in a getting-to-know-you name game last night but whose name I still of course cannot remember is draped across the open doorway of the room across the hall from us, shouting over the first thirty seconds of whatever song someone in there is playing on a laptop.

"I mean, it's just stupid. Like, what example does it set where the first book we're assigned to read in college, BEFORE college, even, we're not even tested on? Not that I WANT to take a test, right? But it's, like—"

We got a letter from the school about a month ago saying all incoming freshmen had to read this book *The Silk-Maker's Assistant,* as an "introduction to our life in the Liberal Arts." I read it and I guess a lot of other people did too. Anyway, it hasn't been mentioned in any of our orientation seminars and there probably will never be a grade given. A lot of people are furious about their time being wasted and I think they are starting to realize that college may not be a hallowed academic proving ground where their finely honed MLA-citation skills will place them at the head of the pack. People are already pissed at the school, but I'm not. I am just happy they accepted a transcript that's a Frankenstein's monster of grades from different high schools. I'm just happy to be away.

My roommate is down in the laundry room but on his desk he has this book someone clearly gave him as a going-away-to-college present. It's this graphic-novel-style thing called *I Got In, Now What?: Getting the Most out of the Best Years of Your Life.* I was leafing through it while I was putting off sitting down to write this, and in it, an amiable slacker guy whose beard is indicated by six black lines jutting out from his chin advises the reader to "just make mistakes!" I took his advice, without ever actually hearing his advice and a full two years before college, and made definitely the biggest mistake of my life. Probably a bigger mistake than most people's biggest mistake of their lives. My brother started college two years before me, and he told me that the kids you're friends with that first week of college you will not end up being friends with in the long run, for whatever reason. In a month, when we're not friends anymore, I'm going to call or e-mail the kids I've been hanging out with this week (Elon, Roger, Kelsey) and tell them they dodged a bullet.

A big debate in the newspapers and among the TV pundits is whether kids with the money to afford over-the-counter Symnitol will have an advantage over kids who can't afford it, or if schools should just go ahead and administer it to everybody. I think I'm sort of a unique case, and I also think who can and can't afford it is the least of their worries, but they don't know that yet. Before I leafed through my roommate's book and before I sat down to write this I pulled a hundred bucks out of the ATM in the laundry room and I took that down to the pharmacy and got fourteen Symnitol, enough to keep me up consequence-free for two weeks. To tell you the truth I can kind of already not-sleep without it, and by getting this down I guess I'm hoping to end that.

Anyway, two weeks seems like a long time. I bet you all I really need is tonight.

s Harrison regain the ability of an un-handicapped
he is freed from his handicaps, but he also seems to defy
hysics. What do you think the author is trying to imply
ness vs. equality?

You must include a cover page and bibliography.

<u>ALL CITATIONS IN PROPER MLA FORMAT!!!!!</u>

1

I've got a system to keep people from seeing what I'm drawing.

A thousand cartoons and TV shows and teen movies would lead you to believe that when you're drawing something at your desk in school, a pretty girl is going to say "What are you drawing?" and you'll tell her and she'll go "That's neat" and your artistry will reveal to her the secret sensitivity in your soul and she'll leave her football-player boyfriend for you. These cartoons and TV shows and teen movies are wrong.

In my experience, a pretty girl never sees you drawing and goes "You're an amazing artist." In my experience a pretty girl sees you drawing and, if she says anything at all, she goes, "Wow, you're a really good drawer." Not drawer like where you put socks, but *draw-er*. Guys who are good at basketball are not described as excellent throwers, and dudes who are good at guitar are not called really good strummers, but somehow I'm a really good draw-er.

And the experience does not change based on what it is she catches you drawing in the margins of your math notebook or whatever. No matter how well you're drawing it, there's nothing good you can be drawing. You can't win. If you're drawing superheroes, that looks nerdy. If you're drawing landscapes or things girls might actually like, like animals, that looks girly. If you're drawing the female figure, you're a pervert. If you're drawing the male figure, you're gay. If you're drawing superheroes and you haven't gotten around to drawing the masks or capes or whatever yet, you're gay. Do yourself a favor: Don't start with the muscles. Start with the rocketpack and work your way out. You'll still be nerdy, but everybody knew that about you already. I mean, come on: you're DRAWING.

And those "how-to-draw-comics" books? Fuck those books. Everybody saw those in their Scholastic book orders in second grade and now they assume I just ordered enough of those books, and that anyone could draw this well if they'd done the same. Well, they're a little right. I did order like two of those books. And the first thing they teach you is this system of lines and shapes, to sketch out the bodies first before you fill in the details. Basically what you have before you start having anything that looks like anything is a page full of what looks like basketballs and potato sacks. The basketball-looking things are eventually gonna be heads and the potato sacks are eventually gonna be torsos, but when I was drawing based on those books, the guidelines would never really erase right and it always looked like all my characters' limbs were built around a sack of potatoes with a superhero insignia printed on it, or like they'd just been nailed in the face with a superheated basketball. Anyway, the point is, fuck those books.

There's this kid, Tony DiAvalo, who always makes a big show of being the kid who draws in class. He'll use whatever time is left over at the end of the period and pull out his special pencils and his special pencil sharpener and this big fucking drawing pad and just start.

He's good, I guess. Probably even good enough to justify all the supplies. But it's just so goddamn showoff-y, and the things he picks to draw are just so inane. It's all pop-culture stuff, never anything original. It's always, like, one of those cartoon M&Ms except the M&M is wearing a doo-rag and smoking a joint and he's written something underneath the M&M like "HUSTLIN'." Kids think it's hilarious. And I guess, if pressed, he would point to that joint and doo-rag as his "originality." He'd probably have you believe he's as original as someone who fills their notebooks with things they made up. All I know is he draws to be seen drawing, and he draws what people want to see. I guess I take back the statement that there's *nothing* good you can be drawing: everybody seems to think preexisting cartoon characters smoking weed and counting money is pretty hilarious, and a good thing to hang in your locker.

One time his showiness got him in trouble and he got busted. Mrs. Cartwright the Spanish teacher saw three or four kids huddling around his pad in the last ten minutes of class when people are supposed to be working on their Spanish free-writing. They were behaving the way people usually do around Tony DiAvalo's drawing pad, which is high-fiving each other, and Tony, and saying "Sick!" That's way more excited than anybody ever is about Spanish free-writing, so Mrs. Cartwright rushed over, and saw on Tony's pad an almost-finished depiction of Tommy from *Rugrats* as Scarface, complete with giant mountain of cocaine. She sent everybody back to their desks except for Tony, who she sent to the office, where he was written up for "advertising drug paraphernalia." So now his M&Ms and his Spongebobs go jointless, though they're still "HUSTLIN'."

While I don't pull out the big fucking pad, it's not like I go behind a curtain or anything, either. I don't make a big show of hiding what I'm drawing. That's just as bad. I don't cup my hand around the part of the notebook page or worksheet-back I'm drawing on. Made that mistake before. It just makes you look guilty. Someone is inevitably going to ask and you can't say no because then it looks like you're hiding something and when you do show them whatever you're drawing it's going to be interpreted with suspicion because it looks like you were hiding something. If this happens and what you're drawing happens to be a girl, the kid you show it to will think it's a girl in your class that you have a crush on. If this happens and you're drawing a gun, the kid will think you want to shoot up the school. So I don't hide it. Or I don't make it look like I'm trying to hide it. Being super-obvious about hiding something is almost showing off. It's almost worse. It's like this fragile-genius thing I think would be disgusting. Like girls in the back of English class being very obvious about the fact that they're writing tortured poetry. No one cares.

And that's the thing, is that no one cares. No one cares but they will ask anyway, in this detached way, "What are you drawing?" and you know just by how they ask that they don't care, and you wonder what the point is of explaining, because they don't care and when you explain they won't understand or even bother to try, but you'll look like a creep if you don't answer but you're so upset by the fact of their even asking in this half-baked way that by the time you do answer you'll come off like a huffy know-it-all, guaranteed, every time. So better, for everyone, to be subtle. Saves you from coming off weird and saves them their I-barely-give-a-shit-anyway energy.

I don't get absorbed. I don't hunch over and curl my tongue up like I'm super-concentrated. The time between when you're finished with your work and class gets out would seem like the best time, because you can concentrate the most, but it's actually the worst. I draw while the teacher is talking, because then everybody's looking up at the front of the classroom, or at least they're supposed to be. I look up periodically, just like everybody else. I jot down notes occasionally, just like everybody else. Every so often my pencil drifts over and draws the jawline of a face. Then it returns to its place and writes "GILDED AGE 1870–1890." Then it drifts over again and draws a nose. Then it goes back and writes "COINED BY MARK TWAIN IN BOOK OF SAME NAME." Then it puts a pair of sunglasses on the nose. I'm into sunglasses recently. They're not as risky as eyes.

When there's not a good reason for me to have my pencil up, I put it away. When that empty five to ten minutes at the end of class comes around where weaker men do their drawing and end up being interrogated by popular girls and pushy dudes, I pull out a book. I try to make it a book we were assigned, too. Fewer questions that way.

"What were you drawing?" somebody asks me when I'm four pages into *The Great Gatsby*, which we just went up to the front of the room to get our copies of.

"Huh?" I look up. Eric Lederer is standing over my desk.

"When Mrs. Amory was talking about our independent essay assignment. You were drawing something."

"Oh yeah. It's nothing."

Eric Lederer and I have never talked, I don't think. All I know about him is he looks like a nerd, turns everything in super-on-time if not early, and knows every answer to every question always and is not shy about raising his hand to prove it. Which makes him a nerd I guess. Cecelia Martin must know more about him than I do, because she's looking at him like he just blew up a school bus and whispering to two girls next to her across the room. Looks like something along the lines of "That guy just blew up a school bus."

"Can I see?" he asks. Having never paid that much attention to him, I haven't until just right now noticed that there's something strange about him. It takes me a second but I realize what it is: he's standing really still. Right in front of my desk, both feet planted. No one stands this awkwardly sure of themselves except characters in my drawings, staring straight ahead with their arms at their sides, because when they start to move around I start to realize that those drawing books might have a point about form and motion, even if what their tips usually get me is a bunch of basketball-burned sack-bodied heroes.

"Sure," I say. I open my notebook. Folded up inside is the bright orange sheet with the criteria for our independent essay assignment. The bright orange color will be a big help when I'm digging through my backpack the night before the essay is due trying to find the criteria so I know what the hell to write, the whole time swearing to myself I'm going to get some sort of organization thing going, but knowing I won't as long as teachers keep printing the important stuff on brightly colored paper that stands out even when it's shoved into my backpack with a roughness that says "I'll never need this again!"

I smooth out the paper and hand it to Eric. In the bottom right-hand corner of the page, underneath big bold letters that say "WORKS CITED IN PROPER MLA FORMAT!!!" two men in suits and dark sunglasses are restraining a cybernetic caveman with electrified lassos.

"Nice monkey," I expect Eric to say. Even with the best intentions people always get what I'm drawing wrong, and admittedly the caveman looks kind of monkey-ish.

"Nice cyborg," Eric says.

"Thanks," I say.

"Is this going to be a comic book?" he asks.

"No," I say, "I was just doodling."

"Oh," Eric says.

I was trying to be dismissive because Eric being genuinely interested seems about as bad as Bret Embler or Carter Buehl being mock-interested. Here somebody across the room is staring at him like he blew up a bus, and I wonder if he has a reputation that I don't know about that's rubbing off on me just by being seen talking to him that will get me lots more attention from idiots. But I may have embarrassed myself just as much by using the word "doodling." I look around, sort of like "does anyone know this kid? I don't," and see that Cecelia and her friends are still looking at Eric like, "That's him, Officer, he's the one who laughed when those kids who thought they were going to school went to Heaven instead."

"You know that kid that always draws cartoon characters?" Eric says.

"Tony. Yeah." He's going to suggest Tony and I would make good friends since we both draw. Lindsay Skinner once told me Tony and I should be "drawing buddies." Lindsay will never know what that remark cost her, and what it cost her was me asking her out, something I had been psyching myself up to do for weeks until the "drawing buddies" comment. So I didn't get to stand in front of Lindsay's locker and stutter out one of the eighty-five variations on "Do you wanna go do something sometime" I'd been weighing the pros and cons of, and Lindsay didn't get to shoot me down.

"Do you think he's good?"

"Tony's alright, yeah."

"Oh," Eric says, the same way he said it when I told him I wasn't drawing a comic book. "I think he's awful."

"Really?" I look around, this time to see if any of Tony's friends are around. Then I realize Tony doesn't really have friends, just what I like to think of as freak-show admirers.

"Yeah," Eric says. "He never draws anything original. You originated these characters, right?"

"I mean, they're just . . . y'know . . . doodles, but yeah."

"I think that's great," Eric says. "I couldn't draw anything, original or otherwise, if my life depended on it."

"Yeah?" I say. "That sucks."

"It does," Eric says. He folds the sheet back up the way it was and gives it back to me.

The bell rings. Eric hustles back to his seat to get his stuff. I throw my notebook and *The Great Gatsby* in my bag and I'm out the door when one of Cecelia's friends, Jen, catches up with me.

"Hey," Jen says. "Do you . . . talk to that kid?"

I shrug. "I dunno," I say. "Not really."

"Oh," she says, "never mind," and starts off down the hallway.

Eric comes out of the classroom, his backpack way too high on his back.

"See you tomorrow," he says. "I know it's not a comic, but you should consider trying your hand at one. Seems like you have the chops, drawing-wise, along with the originality to not just sketch other people's copyrighted material plus drugs."

"It's not a comic, but, uhm," I say. "It's actually a movie trilogy and a series of novels."

"Awesome," Eric says, breaking his weird stillness to hop just a little on his toes. It's geeky but it's pretty much the way I'd want somebody to react if they were the first person I told I was planning a movie trilogy and a series of novels. Eric is the first person. He says "awesome" again and we go off to fourth period in opposite directions.

"What's it about?"

Eric is standing over me again the next day towards the end of third period. No "hi" or "what's up" or anything, like our conversation from yesterday never ended.

"The movie trilogy and series of novels."

"It's sort of a lot to like, go into," I say. "You know the loading dock by the auditorium?"

"Yes," he says.

"I eat lunch over there," I tell him.

"Okay," he says. "Fifth-period lunch?"

"Yep," I say.

"Good," he says all conspiratorial like we're planning a high-stakes daylight robbery. "Good."

When I round the corner of the auditorium, Eric is sitting cross-legged on the concrete loading dock in direct sunlight, his lunch spread out in front of him.

"Aren't you hot?" I say.

"Hmm?"

"Aren't you hot?" I say. "I usually sit in the shade."

At lunchtime, the way the sun hits the school there's a big wedge of shadow on one side of the dock. It's cool up against the brick and easier to read over there.

"Oh, right," he says. "Thanks."

I don't know why he's thanking me, I didn't really do it for him. The truth is he's so pale that in the sunlight he sort of hurts to look at.

He starts packing up his lunch to move. There's four or five little Tupperware containers and something wrapped in tinfoil. He puts them all in a small paper bag and moves toward the shade.

"So?" he says.

I start unwrapping my lunchroom burrito. I have two chili-cheese burritos and a fountain Dr. Pepper. I remember coming to high school when the fact that they had soda seemed like a huge deal. The thrill has worn off but I still get it every day.

"It starts with this scientist who works for the government. He invents these cybernetic modifications for soldiers. His technology ends up causing the deaths of millions of people. Then one day he stumbles upon the technology to make time travel possible, and he knows that if the government gets their hands on it, they'll make things even worse. Then he realizes that he can actually use the technology to go back and prevent those millions of people being killed. But the government busts in just as he's about to go and there's a shootout and he ends up getting sent too far back in time, to the Stone Age, through a temporal distortion."

I take a bite of my burrito. They're pretty messy, but I've figured out how to eat them so not too much stuff leaks out one end.

"Then in the Stone Age . . ." I won't repeat the rest here but there's cybernetic cavemen and a race to an energy crystal at the heart of the universe and the dead and the living keep switching places. When I finish I realize I've never said the whole thing out loud before, or any of it, really. Then I realize I forgot a bunch of things.

"That's dynamite," Eric says. "Really." In the time it's taken me to tell the whole thing he's worked his way through four of the five Tupperware containers (string beans, some kind of potatoes, spinach, fruit salad) and half of what was wrapped in the aluminum foil, which turns out to be a pork chop sandwich.

"Who packs your lunch?" I ask.

"I do," he says, and I remember I have a lunch.

"Leftovers?" I ask.

"No," he says. "I cook."

I expect he'll talk now so I can eat without it being awkward but he doesn't, he just sort of stares straight ahead. I eat anyway, and when I'm done I chew on the rim of my Styrofoam cup.

"What if the scientist—?" he says.

"What if the scientist what?" I say.

He shakes his head. The bell rings.

Wednesday in English Mrs. Amory splits us into groups for group projects. When she announces that Eric is in the same group as Cecelia, Cecelia sighs and looks at Jen and her other friend Teresa. She goes up to talk to Mrs. Amory when we're all supposed to be getting together with our groups. After Cecelia and Mrs. Amory are done talking in very hushed tones, Mrs. Amory calls Eric and Ashlyn Taylor up and tells them they'll be switching groups. My group is Chris White, Alicia Henry, and some girl whose name I always forget but I think might be in choir. Alicia has already divided the project up into four equal sections, assigned one to each of us, and written her e-mail address on three identical-sized strips of notebook paper so we can just e-mail her our sections when we're done and she'll assemble them all in a nice little binder before the due date. She actually says "nice little binder." We all just give in to how badly she wants to get into a good college and go back to our desks with lots of class time to spare.

I'm almost done with *The Great Gatsby* and if we don't get assigned something else soon, I'll have to start reading my own books at the end of class, which I would enjoy except for the questions about what I'm reading and why I'm reading it. Getting asked what book you're reading isn't as bad as getting asked what you're drawing. What you're drawing is coming right from your head onto the page, it's all you, but if a book you're reading looks particularly nerdy, like it has a guy straddling a dragon on the cover, or when you start to describe it to the person asking you realize it sounds particularly nerdy, you can always defuse it by tacking ". . . it sucks" to the end of your description. But then the question becomes "So why are you reading it?" Like, people stop reading assigned books once they realize they suck, they stop reading on page two if page one was too dense or too gay or too historical, so the fact that you're pressing on with a sucky book that no one is even forcing you to read is now a red flag.

Mostly people ask what your book is because they're worried it's something we were assigned when they were ditching out to go huff with some friends they have who go to Catholic school downtown, and they don't think that just because they missed one day means they have any less of a right to know what books they're supposed to half-try to read and give up on for being too dense, gay, and historical.

Eric never comes over to me. He just nods when he catches my eye.

"What if the scientist COULDN'T return to the present?"

Eric is sitting in the shade of the loading dock when I go there after the cafeteria.

"He sends the cavemen back to the present to do his bidding, but why can't he just go back and lead them himself?"

"Because the time-proof signals he sends the cavemen in the present need to get intercepted by the Temporal Ranger—"

"I know. I know he needs to stay in the past for the story to work. But what I'm saying is, there ought to be a reason he has to stay."

Eric looks at me with wide eyes, expecting something, like as long as I don't hit him, this whole thing will be very exciting.

"Like—"

He jumps before the words are even out of my mouth.

"Like what if, unbeknownst to him the government has created a clone of him in the present and the clone him has invented an apparatus to prevent the real him from coming back? And what if . . . well, here, let me show you."

He takes his math book out of his backpack, opens it, and a folded sheet of paper falls out. He unfolds it, and it just keeps unfolding until there's a diagram spread out in front of us. It's covered in words like "scientist" and "Temporal Ranger" and "government." Question marks are everywhere. Things are circled and connected to each other with arrows. It looks like a football play drawn on the blackboard in the locker room in a sports movie, except the players are words I've had in my head for the six months since I came up with this idea. Plus some new ones I don't recognize, like "Dream Spider" and "O.M.N.I." and "Wolfpack Genetically Modified Not To Feel Fear."

"Jesus," I say.

"I got sort of excited about your idea. I thought about it a lot and I sort of assembled this last night. If there's anything in here you don't like, that's fine, it's your idea, but if there's anything you do like, it's all yours. Anyway, the thing I find hard to buy about the caveman troopers is their human behavior. It seems right now they're your average everyday cyborg, only hairier. I mean, isn't the fun of cavemen that they're cavemen?"

By the time the bell rings the world of this has tripled in size. We barely touch our lunches.

"I think this is too big for three movies," Eric says as he slips on his too-high backpack.

"Even with the novels filling in the gaps?"

"Even then."

"Yeah, I was thinking the same thing."

"Also I don't think the title *TimeBlaze: An EVILution* necessarily applies anymore."

"Yeah. But I don't know what else we'd call it . . ."

"Don't worry about it," Eric says. "The title is the least important part."

I spend all sixth and seventh period drawing. I've finished *Gatsby* so I just say fuck it and draw through the last five minutes of class both periods. I cover worksheets front and back, graded-

and-handed-back tests, and most of the school-picture order form we got in homeroom.

Eric spends the next two periods making a list of possible titles, which are the least important part.

It's not until I get home that I realize I'm starving.

The next morning when my dad is driving me to school I think the school parking lot would be a good place for The Committee to attack. The Committee is the government agency Dr. Praetoreous used to work for that's now pursuing him through time. They are ultra-secret, their motives are unclear, their funding is unlimited, and it's very likely they're connected to some ancient architects-behind-every-great-historical-disaster-type society. (Eric and I have decided the scientist's name should be Dr. Praetoreous.)

The Committee decides to kill Dr. Praetoreous back when he's a teenager, before he can do them any harm, so under the protection of the Temporal Ranger, an immortal avatar Dr. Praetoreous accidentally awakened with his TimeBlaze technology, they send a legion of bio-engineered AltraTroops back in time to carry out the task. Dr. Praetoreous erased his own history, but they've somehow gained the name of his high school and the year he graduated so they're going to eradicate everyone at his high school just to be sure they get him.

The troops timejump onto the marching band practice field. They're cloaked, but there's hundreds of them so the grass moves in this unnatural way as it gets trampled by a legion of invisible feet.

One of the troops sends out an electromagnetic pulse. Simultaneously every car in the parking lot dies. They're all new, people's sixteenth-birthday gifts, so they won't run without a million computers working right inside them and the electromagnetic pulse just took those out. Everyone's green parking pass hanging on their rearview mirror is like a toe-tag on their freshly killed cars.

At the same time, every cell phone in everyone's pocket winks off. Kids text messaging in the back of class are cut off in the middle of their thoughts. Their iPods and PSPs and BlackBerries all become bricks in the same second.

The troops take the doors with extreme precision, fearing Dr. Praetoreous may have forseen their attack somehow and protected his young self with a battery of dinosaur-mounted Plasma Calvary sitting right outside the school library, or counterinsurgent nano-mines that will release a million self-replicating mecha-wasps as soon as the enemy cracks the door to the teacher's lounge. But there's nobody: just teachers and kids and lockers and soda machines and plastic furniture, and the AltraTroops go through them all, fist-cannons blazing blue.

Through the chaos and screaming kids walks The Man. Skinny with close-cropped hair, a black suit, a black tie, and black sunglasses. He is the seeming head of The Committee. He's a hologram, given weight and mass when necessary by The Legitimacy Engine, a technology the teenage Praetoreous will invent one year from today, if he lives. No one has ever seen The Man in the flesh, no one knows if there's even flesh to be seen. Cannon discharge rips through him doing no damage, just passing through his unwrinkled suit and out the other side to incinerate a hand-painted homecoming poster. He strides into the attendance secretary's office and punches a few keys on the keyboard. He wants to know who's absent.

Utilizing sub-thought communication, he signals small battalions of AltraTroops who scatter through the surrounding neighborhoods. Kids faking sick watching TV in their living rooms scream as the troops take out their sliding-glass patio doors. Kids who really are sick get the waiting-room magazines blown out of their hands as troops level their doctors' offices with concussion grenades. A kid who looks a lot like Bret Embler is still asleep with a baseball cap on in bed next to his Catholic-school girlfriend when rocket boots scatter the red tile roof of his house in the hills and crash into his bedroom. There's no blood: the fist-cannons' anti-matter fire just makes it so things don't exist.

My dad laughs at something the satellite-radio DJ says about the band Supertramp, then he tells me to have a good day and I hop out of the Jeep. As I walk into school, I imagine cannon discharge passing harmlessly through me.

I tell Eric about this scene at lunch. He likes it, he says, except we could never storyboard it. We both agree that if we ever put it down on paper someone would see it and we'd be "red-flagged" and suspended like Carl Whiteman, who they found with a "hit list" of kids he thought "deserved it" freshman year.

Eventually, Eric and I agree, Dr. Praetoreous will go back and counteract the high school hit and all the kids will be safe, restored to their places in the timestream whether or not time and space have missed them all that much. But in order for that to happen, it had to actually happen at one point in the timestream, so Eric and I both agree that it did. And our high school works because Dr. Praetoreus would be our same age at this year in time. We sort of hope we were born late enough in history that by the time we are in our forties and fifties "existence engineer" and "clone wrangler" will be viable career paths.

"You should come over to my house this weekend," I tell Eric at the end of lunch on Friday. "To work on this."

"Absolutely," Eric says. Because Cecelia Martin and Carter Buehl and people like that, they hang out. Eric and I work.

My brother's friends are inexplicably dressed as ninjas and jumping around the front yard when Eric shows up at eight thirty on Friday night. Or rather they have been jumping around the front yard dressed up as ninjas and Eric shows up as soon as they're gone. He said he was going to come over at seven thirty and he shows up at eight thirty all sweaty.

"I circled the block a few times," Eric says. "There were ninjas."

"They weren't really ninjas," I say. "Just my brother and his idiot friends."

"I know," Eric says. "I just didn't want to—um—"

I guess a bunch of seniors dressed as ninjas swearing and kicking each other in the chest for an hour before peeling away in their cars could be scary to some people, but I'm used to it.

"My dad's on a date," I tell Eric. "We pretty much have the run of the place."

There are pizza boxes stacked four deep on the kitchen counter. "We have pizza on Fridays," I tell Eric. "You want some?"

"No thanks," he says. "I ate."

"There's sodas and stuff in the fridge." I open the fridge. Somebody else being around makes me really look at what's inside, and it really is just sodas and stuff. I try to think if there's anything in our cabinets that makes it look like we cook or my dad cooks or we eat anything besides takeout, and I don't think there is. We have a "chip cabinet" and a "cracker cabinet." We have a lot of cabinets.

"I was thinking about it," Eric says, "when I was walking around the block, and I think *TimeBlaze: An EVILution* can still work. Can I have one of those waters?"

I hand Eric a water bottle and get myself a Dr. Pepper.

"I just think it has to be the full title. So you know how *Star Wars* is *Star Wars Episode IV: A New Hope*? In our case the titles would go *TimeBlaze: An EVILution: Crisis Endpoint*."

"What's *Crisis Endpoint*?"

"That would be the name of that particular part. Like *Lord of the Rings: The Two Towers*."

"Oh, right."

"It's just an example, but do you like it?"

"Yeah," I say, "I like it."

"Why do they dress like ninjas?"

"I dunno. They're retarded?"

"Maybe it's to jump people," he says.

"I don't think they jump anybody. They're my brother's friends from church."

"Those kids go to church?" Eric says.

"Yeah. It's like this youth church or whatever. My family's not religious, my brother just goes because his friends do."

"So they're religious kids?"

"They're not anything kids."

Eric looks out at my pool. "I think maybe they jump people."

"I dunno," I say.

We play video games in my room. A fighting game my brother rented. Eric's terrible.

"Look at this guy! Who needs a sword that big?" Eric says about my character, a skinny guy with long blond hair in an admiral's uniform who is obliterating Eric's character with a big fuck-off sword. Eric's character is a disembodied eyeball on top of a purple whirlwind.

"It's like a surfboard! Beyond your bigger broadswords, size just becomes a disadvantage. It's bigger than he is!"

The admiral's sword glows blue and slashes the purple whirlwind, dealing the eyeball serious damage.

"And how does that hurt me? You didn't even hit anything resembling flesh!"

The eyeball goes tumbling off the cliff level's precipice when the admiral lands a surprisingly effective kick with his red slipper.

"You know who my guy looks like?" I say. "Emma Tomlinson."

"You're totally right," Eric says. "Do you like her?"

"Ew! No."

"No, I didn't mean—I didn't mean romantically, I meant just do you think she's okay."

"What's to like? She never talks."

"Good! Yeah! Me too! I think she's an albino."

"I think you're right."

"And her whole family comes to pick her up from school. Her mom AND her dad AND her two little sisters and they all look exactly like her."

"It's like they sent a homeschooled kid to regular school."

"Have you ever known any homeschoolers?"

"There are some next door. One time we went on vacation and

they picked up our mail for us and I had to go get it when we got back and their whole house smelled like . . . I dunno. Oatmeal? It was creepy in there. I can't put my finger on it."

"We don't talk to people. Do you think people think we're creepy?"

"I talk to people!"

"I've never seen you talk to anybody in English."

"Yeah, well, not in English. Why don't you focus on the game? I'm killing you here."

We're halfway through another match. I'm thrashing Eric again. I'm a tiny Asian schoolgirl with two razor fans. Eric's a half-man, half-Zeppelin.

A couple seconds go by where it's just the sound of my girl squealing every time she lands a knee or a fan on Eric's character, and his character harrumphing.

Then Eric says, "You know who my guy looks like?" His guy puffs up like a blimp and rockets into the Asian girl, actually a pretty good move I'm sure he got completely by accident. "Patti Helzburg."

"Patti is fatter and has a bigger mustache."

Eric cracks up. We rip on people from school for a while as I beat him but not as badly, then we go downstairs to get sodas.

"How long have your parents been divorced?" Eric says.

"Since I was like nine."

"Is it strange having your dad go on dates?"

"No, I'm used to it or whatever."

"I would think that would be strange. Here it is Friday night, your dad is on a date. A lot of kids our age are on dates too. If your dad took his date to the movie theater, there's a very strong chance he took his date to see the same movie kids our age took their dates to."

"I don't think they're going to the movies," I say, shutting the cabinet too hard.

"Sorry, I didn't mean to—" Eric says. "Sorry. I'm sorry."

I shrug.

"Do you want me to leave?"

"What? No!"

"Okay," Eric says. "I'll have a Dr. Pepper, I think." He opens the fridge and grabs a can. "I was thinking . . . I was thinking about the soundtrack, too."

"Soundtrack?"

"For the movie. The first one."

"Oh yeah?"

"Yeah. I was thinking it'd be cool if it had exclusively industrial music. Like Throbbing Gristle, Bauhaus . . ."

I have to admit I don't know who those bands are.

"Oh. They're from the seventies and eighties. I think they would fit really well with the tone of the first movie. I was really interested in industrial music for a while."

"Cool. I've been thinking about it too. I was thinking, I dunno, more modern stuff, like, uhm, The Earnest February, or Forty Guns, or The Boy Who Cried Sparrow."

"UGH. I hate The Boy Who Cried Sparrow. I can't stand them. I absolutely, I mean, I can't stand them."

"Okay! Jeez. They don't have to . . . we don't have to put them on the soundtrack."

"I'm sorry if you like them, maybe that's where we part company, because I think they're completely overrated. Like, I get it, their singer went to college. Those lyrics could only be considered deep by a sixth-grader. And their arrangements? Pabulum."

"Fine. Wow."

We start back upstairs. I have no idea what *pabulum* means, or really what "arrangements" are, at least in relation to music. I barely expected Eric to know what I was talking about much less have such a violent reaction. It's one part scary and one part hilarious to see him so enthusiastic and negative.

"Maybe we're putting the cart before the horse," Eric says when we're back upstairs, "thinking about the soundtrack before we even have the script necessarily, or the whole thing planned out."

I really think about it, then I say, "No. I don't think so. I think it's important to know what kind of mood we're trying to have, y'know?"

"Good," Eric says, "I don't think so either. You know who your guy looks like?" he says. "Tony DiAvalo." He smiles.

We go to bed at three. Eric unrolls his sleeping bag and goes through a whole nighttime ritual. I feel like he's never spent the night at somebody's house before. He has pajamas. Not, like, feety pajamas or anything, but clothes that are specifically for sleeping. An oversize T-shirt with some microchip-company logos, and a pair of gym shorts.

"Do you want a pillow?" I ask.

"Oh, right," he says. "I forgot my pillow. Knew I forgot something."

"No problem," I say, and throw him one from my bed.

We talk about the opening chase sequence through feudal Japan for a little while longer. When discussing the extra-fat Japanese warlord Praetoreous escapes from via riddles, we draw numerous comparisons to Patti Helzburg then we both go silent and I fall asleep pretty quickly.

"FAGGOT PATROL! FAGGOT PATROL!"

I wake up to screaming out in front of the house. It sounds like my brother's friend Alan's sister Cathy.

"Shut the fuck up Cathy you bitch!" my brother yells in what he calls his "wifebeater" voice, which is basically the world's worst bad Southern accent. "Shut the fuck up!"

There's a loud smacking sound. Cathy screams then laughs like a witch.

I sit up. The TV is on. Eric's awake, sitting up in his sleeping bag, playing Threat Monster: Blue, the game we were playing before. Or at least I think he is. It's two characters I haven't seen before, and a totally different level. A panda in a mechanized body-suit fights a kabuki guy whose right arm is a crossbow in a vertical neon city at night.

"Are you the panda or the kabuki guy?" I say.

"Oh, hey," Eric says. "The ninjas are back." Eric leans forward to turn the TV off.

"Don't worry about it," I say, and he leans back and keeps playing. "Did they wake you up?"

"No. I was up. I woke up earlier. They just got back. I'm the panda. Don't worry, I saved your game and started a new one." The TV is muted. The controller buttons click.

"RAPE! RAPE! RAPE!" my brother shouts out on the lawn.

"Cathy, stop raping him! Stop RAY-PING him," Alan screams in a terrible British accent. "He's moi MATE!"

"Your brother and his friends sure know how to have fun on a Friday night," Eric says.

"It's Saturday morning now," I say. It is. The sun's starting to come up behind my blinds.

We stay up until like nine playing with all the new characters Eric's unlocked and then he walks home. I sleep the whole rest of the day and try to ignore Cathy and my brother in my brother's room laughing and yelling and whatever else all day.

I don't know anybody who thinks Cecelia Martin is cute. Her and Jen Ackerman and Teresa Saylor make up this little clique of I don't know exactly what you would call them. Goth girls? They wear baggy black jeans and spiked belts and black T-shirts with Invader Zim on them and black eyeliner and their hair is always dyed in chunks and colors that make it look like they did it with highlighter, which they may have.

Cecelia walks next to me out of English on Monday.

"Do you hang out with Eric Lederer?" she says. Her voice is too high for her body.

"Yeah . . ." I say.

"Oh, like, just so you know," she says, "he's weird. Like, really weird."

"Okay."

"He was like obsessed with me for a while. He saw on my Namespot page that we liked the same music or something, so he thought we were like soul mates or something."

"Huh," I say. "That is weird."

"He told me . . ." she says.

"Told you what?"

"Anyway," she says, "he's weird. I think he might be like one of those school shooters or something."

"Why do you think that?"

"He was like obsessed with The Boy Who Cried Sparrow," she says. "Like obsessed."

"You think he's a school shooter 'cause he really likes a band?"

"You don't understand," she says. "He's weird."

"He told me he hates them."

"I told you. Weird," Cecelia says. "I gotta go to Spanish. I just thought you should know."

"Uhm, okay."

I head down the stairs and Cecelia turns around and heads for Spanish, where her Spanish name is probably Noche or Muerta or Mariposa, because those girls are either obsessed with death or cute things. Like, obsessed.

So he got excited when he found out you guys like the same things. That's exciting, and sometimes when that happens if the person who likes the same things as you doesn't turn out to be a complete fucking simpleton who thinks she's enlightened just because her belt has spikes on it, you and that person will become friends and the two of you will chart out whole literal galaxies on the backs of worksheets, with infinite time to flesh out what you've charted. If it turns out the person isn't that cool, it just might sour you on that thing you both like. So I get why Eric now hates The Boy Who Cried Sparrow and I continue to get why no one who doesn't look and behave and think exactly like Cecelia Martin likes Cecelia Martin.

By October we have three notebooks full of concept art for *Time-Blaze*. By this time Dr. Praetoreous, instead of being the main character, is just another player in a universe of characters, including the Praetoreous family (each of whom is actually another version of Dr. Praetoreous in a different timestream, so there's cowboy Praetoreous and postapocalyptic Praetoreous and two-dimensional Praetoreous in a universe rendered in 2D), the Time Squad (the Temporal Ranger's extended posse of villains, rogues, and scoundrels from the outskirts of time), and an entire pantheon of gods drawn from the Greek, Aztec, Indian, and Chinese mythologies who have been summoned by The Man using Dr. Praetoreous's invention known as The Mortalizer. (Aside from cracking the whole time-travel deal wide open, Dr. Praetoreous's strong suit is inventions that make unreal things real, from The Legitimacy Engine all the way up to The Mortalizer.) It helps that Eric knows shit-tons about all these different mythologies, even though all we ever learned about gods in school was a three-week Greek mythology unit in English freshman year, and the time D'andrea Rhys-Phelps, a Jehovah's Witness kid, got so offended by the fact that there was a fortune-telling booth at the school carnival that we had to have a two-hour assembly on religious sensitivity.

I am proud of the way, in this one drawing, the Aztec god Quetzalcoatl seems to be almost 3D, his feathered tail way off in the distance in the bottom right corner of the page and his semi-reptilian head roaring toward you in the top left as The Man stands passively at the top of an ancient South American ruin, directing the newly Mortalized god to go out and fuck shit up.

On Halloween we decide that dressing up and trick-or-treating is for kids so instead we're gonna stay inside and work on merchandising ideas. No detail is too small, we've decided, from the soundtrack to possible directors for the movies to the cover art for the books to the fast-food tie-ins, which we realize is sort of commercial and sell-out-y but we definitely know we're going to have to consider if anybody is going to take on an expensive project like this, especially from two fifteen-year-olds. We've watched enough DVD commentaries to know that money is a big factor.

Eric is going to come over at eight but my brother and his friends are dressed as pirates in the front yard, and Eric doesn't show up until they go off down the block, and by then it's nine thirty.

"Your brother and his friends are seniors" is the first thing Eric says when he gets in the door.

"Yeah, I dunno," I say. "They dress up all the time. Why should Halloween be any different?"

"Are they going to trick or treat?"

"I dunno."

"They're probably going to steal candy from kids."

"I dunno what they're going to do," I say. "You don't have to avoid them. You can just come up when they're out front. They're pretty loud but they're harmless."

Eric doesn't say anything.

We spread paper out on my bedroom floor. Around eleven thirty we go downstairs for sodas.

"What's the grossest way you can think of to die?" I ask Eric.

"Grossest or out-and-out worst?" Eric asks.

"Both, I guess."

"It's the same answer for both. Having your brain eaten away by spiders nesting in your ear canal."

"Eww! That's fucking gross!"

"You asked. It's bad, too, isn't it? Now you go."

"Uhmm . . ."

But before I can think of one (I obviously hadn't thought about it as much as Eric) the front door crashes open. My brother comes in, hair spiked up like an anime character with a red bandanna tied around his neck and a plastic sword tucked into a plastic sheath on his hip. He comes into the kitchen and makes for the fridge. Eric suddenly becomes interested in the cracker cabinet, or pretends to.

"We have any whipped cream?" my brother asks.

"I dunno," I say.

He answers his own question by pulling an aerosol can of whipped cream from the condiment part of the fridge, which is most of the fridge.

"Do you have a house, or . . . ?" my brother says to the back of Eric's head.

"Me?" Eric says, half turning around.

"Yeah, you're over here, like, all the time. Where do I know you from?"

Eric basically has his head in the cracker cabinet between the Original Wheat Thins and the Sour Cream N' Onion Wheat Thins, that's how hard he's avoiding eye contact.

"I dunno," Eric says.

"Operation Chaos!" my brother says.

Operation Chaos was when my brother and his friends watched *Fight Club* fifty times in a row one weekend and decided it was their mission to spread anarchy in our subdivision. I don't know what form it ended up taking, really, just that my brother and Alan both got community service for shoplifting, and my brother came home that weekend with a YIELD sign he then hung on the wall of his bedroom.

"Yeah, that's it!" my brother says. "Darren, check it out, your friend was walking down Mountain Terrace at like three in the morning, right, and Alan and Tits and me were driving down Mountain Terrace and we saw him, so we like start flashing our lights and swerving over and honking like we're gonna hit him, and he FREAKS and jumps into the bushes, so we stop and get out and we thought we lost him, but Tits tripped over his sneaker on the way to the car, so Tits drags him out of the bushes . . ."

"Stop," I say. "No one cares." I don't know if you have ever heard someone describe beating someone else up in the presence of that someone else, not in a cruel way, just in a way that's like it's not supposed to bother that person.

"Man, you should've seen it," my brother says. "It was classic, right?" he says to Eric. "ROIGHT?" he screams in his and Alan's favorite British hooligan put-on accent.

Eric just looks at the kitchen tile.

"No one cares," I say again. "Fuck off!"

"Chee-kee," my brother says, punching me in the shoulder as hard as he can.

"DAN-yul," Cathy shrieks. She's hanging in the front doorway, her breasts apparent in a pirate blouse, wearing heavy makeup. "HURRY UP!"

"I'm COM-ing," my brother shrieks back. He runs out with the whipped cream. Eric and I look at each other.

"They jump people," Eric says.

"He's a retard," I say.

"I got kicked in the stomach by someone named Tits," Eric says.

"They just call him Tits because he's fat."

Eric doesn't say anything. My shoulder hurts where my brother punched me.

"You should have told me they beat you up."

"We weren't friends back then."

"I meant, when you first came over. You knew it was them."

"I didn't want to start anything."

I don't think it's within Eric's power to start anything, but I don't say that. It's also not really within my power to start anything.

"You want to keep working on ideas?" I say.

Eric shakes his head.

"Yeah, me neither." I look out at the pool. I can imagine a thousand kids out there beyond the fence, fucking up and getting into trouble, kids way dumber and less deserving of a good time than Eric and me, and here we are indoors, feeling like weak beat-uppable tools. I say: "You want to get them back?"

"Get them back? How would we go about doing that?" Eric asks. I don't have any idea, but we are two fifteen-year-olds on Halloween and I'm sure deep within our ancestral teenage-boy lizard brains are all sorts of fun ways to cause problems after ten p.m.

What we have on the kitchen counter five minutes later makes it pretty clear we've never gotten revenge on anybody. Half a dozen eggs leftover from two weeks ago when my dad made breakfast for a woman who stayed over on a Saturday night. Processed, individually wrapped yellow cheese slices because I feel like I remember seeing or reading about a prank involving cheese slices somewhere, but maybe it was an art project, not a prank. Some rope from the garage, just in case we have to rappel up or down something. Neither of us knows how to rappel, in fact I've always counted myself lucky that our school doesn't have that rope-climbing thing as part of PE like you see in movies. But rappelling seems like something you do as part of getting really excellent revenge. We could also use the rope to hang somebody in effigy, if we decide to go that way. But again, that's straying into art-project territory.

It also seems like a good time to spray-paint somebody's house or car, but we don't have any spray paint. We have a can of wood-staining stuff from the time my dad painted our deck. It's not even technically paint, and it's heavy as hell. Also, we have some flash-lights.

"It looks like we're going to make an omelet," Eric says, "rappel in through somebody's window, and serve it to them."

"You read my mind," I say. Eric laughs.

We go out the door without much of a plan and everything in a paper grocery bag, becoming two of a ton of kids out tonight with some rotten eggs and bad intentions but probably the only ones with a can of Home Depot store brand chestnut wood stain.

My brother and his friends could be any number of places. They could be hanging out at one of their houses or at somebody else's house. They could be hot-boxing my brother's car in the Sonic parking lot. They could be speeding around in the car after hot-boxing it. They could be hopping out on middle-schoolers and threatening them with plastic pirate swords to make them give up their candy. Cathy could be flashing her boobs at eight-year-olds dressed up like Yu-Gi-Oh characters. And if they aren't doing these things right now they probably will be later. But we know they're not at my house so we decide to go to Alan's house, because it's the only one of his friends' houses I know the address of.

It would take us a year to walk. Eric suggests we take the bus.

"He lives on Desert Wind Drive," I say. "It's over by the—"

"I know where it is," Eric says.

I don't ever take the bus. It's not the city bus, it's this little shut-tle they added to our suburb a couple years ago, I guess to ferry around little old ladies and take kids who can't drive yet to and from the movie theater. When it came out they had this big logo design contest. Tony DiAvalo submitted this winking cartoon bus he was sure was gonna win, but when it didn't he told everybody the city should be glad they didn't pick his design because the whole thing had been a goof and his cartoon was filled with hidden joints and subliminal gang symbols.

"Is your brother going to kick our ass?" Eric says as we wait for the shuttle.

"As long as we don't get caught, they'll probably just chalk it up to it being Halloween. Random prank."

"What prank ARE we going to do?" Eric asks.

I don't know and I tell him we'll figure it out on the bus, which has just pulled up with the winning logo, a boxy little cartoon bird flying in the direction the bus is going, painted on the side. We climb up. It's free so we don't have to put in any money or anything.

When we're climbing on, Eric says, "Hey, Eulalio."

"What's goin' on, man?" says the bus driver, whom I guess is Eulalio.

"You know the bus driver?" I ask as we make our way to the back of the bus, past a couple girls our age dressed as sexy Native Americans, and an old man in jogging clothes.

"Yeah, I take the bus a lot," Eric says.

We take seats at the back of the bus. I'm extra careful with the bag to make sure the can of wood stain doesn't roll over and crush the eggs. The cheese and rope are a buffer. "I mean, besides just egging his house . . . what can we do?"

"I don't know," Eric says. "I've been thinking about it. . . . If we tied an egg to the rope . . ."

"Right . . ." I say.

"Or if we tied the can with some rope . . ."

"Okay . . ."

"And then the cheese . . . The flashlight could . . ."

"Hmm."

"To be honest," Eric says, "I'm just combining all the things we have in my head like some Rube Goldberg contraption."

"Okay, well, the contraption you keep thinking of . . . what does it do?"

"Make omelets."

"Shit." It's the eggs and the cheese. The effect of those two items together makes everything around them seem breakfast-y. And "start your day off right" is not the message we're hoping this prank will send.

"We could stain the eggs brown," Eric says. "When he goes to clean them up he'll think he's been egged with some weird sort of animal's egg as opposed to just a regular chicken's egg."

"I don't think he's going to think that."

"You're right."

We hate to settle for a conventional egging, even though winging eggs at the side of some dude's house would be a first for both of us. Like, with *TimeBlaze*, we are hoping to reinvent the sci-fi/fantasy saga as the world knows it, and with this prank, we are hoping to change pranking forever. Even if no one knows about it and we did just decide to do it with the materials we had on hand, I would be really disappointed if we settled for your typical pitch-eggs-at-stucco-and-bolt, and I'm pretty sure Eric would too. At that point we might as well just be my brother and his friends; in fact, they'd probably come up with something better than that if only because they're meaner than us and willing to go further.

The bus makes a right into Alan's subdivision, The Cliffs At Tapatillo Point. "I mean, if all else fails," I say, "there's no shame in just egging his house."

"Right," Eric says. "Or his car."

Eric signals Eulalio and we get out on the corner of Mountain Terrace and Desert Wind Drive. It's getting later so fewer little kids are out. Knots of older kids are up and down the street with trick-or-treat bags, not quite our age but close. They're rowdier and pushier than the little kids and their costumes are shittier and they don't have parents straggling along behind them. I feel like there's a window after you get too old to trick-or-treat supervised by a parent where you can do it with your friends by yourselves and as long as you push and swear enough and don't try too hard, you can keep getting free candy for a few years. I had a couple years like that in middle school with my friends Ethan and Chung Hoon. One year we were the Monty Python lumberjacks and the next year we were chess pieces. Chung Hoon moved away after that and Ethan went to a different high school. Actually, we did try pretty hard, but we definitely pushed one another and swore, too.

Alan's house is at the end of the cul-de-sac. My brother's car isn't here but Alan's is parked out front, covered in stickers from bands, newer stickers starting to cover old ones of bands Alan's decided he doesn't like anymore.

I get these knots in my stomach when there's even the remote possibility of getting in trouble. I've gotten them since I was a kid. It's not really a guilty feeling, it's more a fear that I'm going to get caught and somebody's going to tell my parents. I get them less since my mom moved away. I have one as we walk up to Alan's house, but it doesn't make me want to stop. It almost makes me want to keep going with whatever it is we're going to do, which will almost certainly be stupid.

"Let's go around back," I say.

"Why?" Eric says.

I shrug. Eric nods. We go around back.

The pool light is on even though it's October. All the lights in the house are off except for what I guess is Alan's bedroom. I know it's Alan's bedroom because through the blinds I can see Alan lying on his bed and a girl is lying across him, going down on him. We were sneaky and quiet before but now we are frozen. The pool filter hums and Alan's got some sort of music on, loud, not the kind of music I think I would put on but what the fuck do I know. Though he's my brother's friend and Eric's tormentor I don't think either of us has ever seen this sort of thing before. I definitely haven't outside of the Internet and I don't know that Eric has, ever. I don't even know if he knows there is such a thing.

"Oh my God," Eric whispers.

The girl is rubbing her boob up and down Alan's cock.

The thing that's weird about it, besides all the things that are obviously weird about it, is that it's real: I know that sounds dumb or oversimple but it's the fact that, like I said, up until this point the only time I've ever seen anything remotely resembling this is in porn, and this is most definitely not porn. Alan is sort of fat and the girl, who I actually think I might recognize, is almost too skinny and they're more dressed than they are naked. Alan has this hoodie on that I recognize from when he forgot it at our house for like a week and it was draped over the chair by the front door, green with white lettering that reads THE WORLD'S BEST FUCK-ING SKATERS, and it's real and if it's happening right now it's happening all over in the backs of normal-looking houses all the time while Eric and I sit indoors and draw. I mean, you hear rumors, even if you're not friends with anyone named in the rumors, but I guess I always figured it was like fights: you know, people say they're going to kick each other's asses but all they really do is meet on the basketball court after school and push each other and call each other "bitch" enough so that nobody will be considered one when they both end up walking away and not actu-ally fighting. Just like fighting is mostly just talk about fighting, I figured sex at our age was mostly just talking about sex. But it really happens. People born not long before me rub each other all over each other in their bedrooms with the music up.

"Let's go around front," Eric says.

It is a good five seconds before either of us moves.

Back around front we're a couple of kids with rotten eggs on Hal-loween and even though we're not dressed as Disney characters and saying "twick or tweat" with adorable speech impediments we might as well be. We're standing on the curb. Eric takes the eggs out of the bag, opens the carton, and looks at them. I grab one and throw it at Alan's house. I guess the driveway is longer than it looks or I am weaker than I already feel because it doesn't even make it. It breaks in front of a red clay pot next to the front door. I am wondering if being so awful at being a teenager that you can't even prank right counts as originality when my brother's car pulls into the cul-de-sac.

Eric struggles to close the egg carton and get it back in the bag. He gives up and drops them to the concrete.

"Well well well," my brother yells out his rolled-down window in his British hooligan voice, "what's all dis den?"

I take off running. Since it's a cul-de-sac, really I'm running towards the people we're trying to get away from.

"DARREN," Eric says. I turn. Eric tilts his head back the way we came, towards Alan's backyard. It's kind of a cool move. I've never seen Eric have a cool move. Then he runs in the direction he nodded. I follow. My brother gives chase, plastic sword thwapping against his thigh. Tits has jumped out on us too, and whoever else was in the car, a couple of dark forms following my brother when I look back over my shoulder. I hope Eric's not planning something stupid like jumping in Alan's pool. I hope somebody tripped over the wood-stain can.

Eric runs around Alan's pool. There's a back gate I didn't notice when we were zoning out on Alan's sex triumph. Eric blasts through the gate, I do too, and we're in a back alley between fences where there's trash bins and a couple of old couches and trampolines. My brother is right behind us.

"Throw eggs at moi mate's house, will you?" He cackles like a fucking demon.

I had no idea this alley was back here. I didn't know we had alleys. We come to what I guess is the end of the block. It looks like a dead end and I'm bracing myself to slow down and take whatever shoulder punches and nut punches and kicks in the gut from Tits are coming to us when Eric cuts into a dark corner and disappears. I run that way. Some steel rods demarcate a place where the alley opens onto a dry wash. Eric scrambles down the sharp gray rocks that look unsteady as hell and, as I find out when I try to scramble down as fast as Eric, actually are unsteady as hell. Rocks clatter against rocks. I fuck my knee up bad a couple of times but manage to stay right behind Eric. Behind me, the thwappings of the sword against my brother's leg get farther and farther apart, and the cackles get less and less demon-ish. Eric hangs a right and climbs out of the wash. He holds his watch up, presses a little button that lights up the face. "We might be able to make this work," he says. As I'm climbing out of the wash a shape flies past me and clatters on the pavement. A plastic sword, still in its sheath. I look over my shoulder. My brother stands panting in the dry wash. It doesn't look like Tits ever even made it down there. They're heavy smokers, of everything.

I try to tell Eric we could probably slow down but before I can he's let his little watch light go out and has jetted down the block we've just climbed up to. Most of the houses are under construction. At the end of the street, another shuttle is just pulling up.

"The eleven fifteen," Eric pants, "right on time!" Its doors open and Eric sprints up the stairs without stopping. I climb on and nod to the driver, who's not Eulalio.

"GO GO GO!" Eric says when he gets to his seat, though he has to see no one's chasing us anymore. The bus pulls away at its own pace.

By now, I imagine the commotion has disturbed what Alan had going on. I don't know if it's a regular thing for him or a one-time full-moon Halloween anomaly, all I know is Alan has been to a place I haven't been to, and I'm really smart and I once heard Alan pronounce the word *especially* like this: "eck-specially." So I guess what I'm trying to say is I'm not sorry.

We sit there catching our breath. I am so out of shape it feels like my body has given up trying to draw air from my underused lungs and is trying to run on a heart full of caffeine and a stomach that only knows Hot Pockets, and it's having a bitch of a time. Still, it's kind of great. We have these characters the Agtranian Berserkers, who jab each other in the chest with big syringes full of superadrenaline before they go into battle, so they're so euphoric they don't give a fuck if they die. As soon as I stop feeling like I'm dying, I start feeling like that.

"Your house won't be safe for a while," Eric says. "We can go to mine."

I've never been to Eric's house. I don't know what I'm expecting. I guess one of those homeschoolers' houses we talked about that one time: weird-smelling and dark and crammed with spelling workbooks and homemade candles, his mom in a dress like a farmer's wife, listening to religious radio. But it's not like that at all. It's normal. Big, even.

"How did you do that?" I say as we walk up the gravel path to Eric's front door. "You were like a fucking ninja."

"I know the neighborhood pretty well."

"Did you live over there or something?"

"No."

Eric takes out his keys and opens the front door.

"Are your parents home?" I whisper.

"Yes, but they're asleep, and their room is upstairs, so don't feel the need to whisper."

"Okay."

Eric gets me a water bottle from the fridge and gets one for himself. His kitchen is cleaner than mine but essentially the same.

"You saved our asses. How did you know where the bus stop was? How did you know the way out of that . . . I mean, I didn't even know we had alleys."

"I walk around at night a lot," Eric says.

"Right, my brother said they saw you that night. Here's the thing: I think we got them back, but I'm not sure we did. I'm not sure we did anything, but it feels like we got them back."

"They had to run," Eric said, "but they never caught us. They were mad and they never got an outlet for their anger. One time I tried to get away from them and couldn't and this time I did. And we probably put a hitch in things for, you know, that guy and . . . his girlfriend."

"Man, right through Alan's backyard . . ." I'm still kind of excited. I mean, I can never go home again, but I'm never outside at night and I'm definitely never running from people at night and just narrowly escaping.

Then I think about Alan's backyard and what we saw back there. I think about it and I'm quiet. Eric's quiet so I figure he's probably thinking about it too.

"Can I tell you something?" Eric says.

"Sure," I say.

Then Eric says, "I can't sleep."

He says it fast and mumbly and quiet like the time I told Sara Eldensparr I liked her. *Ilikeyou. Ican'tsleep.* Like something you've thought about a million ways to sort of cleverly segue into and you get the attention of the person you intend to say it to and in that moment you reach down for your favorite clever segue and it's not there so you just figure "Let's get this over with as fast as possible," and sometimes it's sloppy and they don't understand you but I hear Eric clearly I think.

"Well, don't drink so much caffeine or whatever."

"No. That's not what I mean. I mean I can't sleep. I've never been able to and I don't have to. I am physically incapable of it and don't require it."

"What?"

"Next you're going to ask if I'm joking. I'm not. Then you're going to accuse me of being crazy. I can't speak on that as definitively as I can on the fact that I'm not joking, but I don't think I am. It's been this way since I was born."

"You're serious."

"Yes."

Eric sets his water bottle down on the counter and it lands with a quick series of sounds instead of just one, and that's when I notice he's trembling, which is also a lot like the time I told Sara

Eldensparr I liked her, except all I told Sara Eldensparr was that I liked her, not that I could walk through walls or spit fire or eat bullets out of midair.

"That's impossible."

"I know."

"You can't NOT sleep. I saw a thing about this on the Discovery Channel. While you're sleeping, your body regenerates. If you didn't sleep, you'd die."

"I know."

"And your subconscious mind works a bunch of things out while you sleep. Sometimes apparently you can go to sleep with something on your mind, and when you wake up, you just KNOW the answer, because your brain worked it out without you having to tell it to."

"I know."

"And besides, you're legally insane after seventy-two hours! I saw this on Court TV, this guy used it as his defense in court when he murdered his wife, he had insomnia—"

"Do I seem legally insane?"

"Sort of! You're telling me you don't have to sleep—"

"I CAN'T sleep."

"You're telling me you can't sleep! That seems insane."

"I don't know. I just can't do it and I've never had to and I've never been able to. I've tried. Trust me. I've tried. I don't know."

"Dude." I don't know what to say. Then I think of something. "Prove it."

"It's not a trick I can do. You would just have to sit and watch me not sleep."

"Okay."

"Okay."

We go up to Eric's bedroom. There's a couch and a desk with a computer and a TV with a PlayStation 2 hooked up and three or four bookshelves completely full and a ton of other stuff. There's a bed that looks like it was made up by a Marine, sheets perfect like in a furniture showroom.

"Who sleeps in that bed, then?" I say.

"Not me," Eric says.

It's one in the morning when I settle in to watch Eric not sleep.

"Dude, if you're joking, now would be the time to tell me that you're joking."

"Again: not joking," Eric says, sitting down on the couch. "What do you want to do?"

"I don't know!"

"I mean, while we wait. While I prove it by not sleeping. I rented Bastion Of Heroes, the co-op mode is actually very—"

"No. Sorry. Let's just—" I don't even know what "let's just." I shut up and collapse against the opposite wall of the room and slide down into a sitting position. And I guess I'm willing to stay this way until Eric tells me what his deal is.

I am completely mind-fucked sideways by this. And that's only assuming right up front that it's not true. If what Eric's saying is false, which it has to be, then it makes everything I know about him false, because I cannot imagine a reason for him to tell me this, this absolutely made-up story. It's like when you're taking a standardized test with one of those bubble sheets and you're humming along, filling in the circles the whole way like they show at the top of the sheet, and you go to fill in the answer for question 58 and you realize the next empty circle is 59, you've been one number off for God knows how long, maybe since the teacher flipped over her one-hour egg timer. It might only be one number but now everything is wrong. I do not know him and I do not feel comfortable doing anything with him but sitting and waiting until he falls asleep, and this can all be over, our friendship probably included.

Because you can't just believe somebody, can you? I mean it: kids exaggerate how many people the party bus they're renting this weekend can accommodate and the length of their family vacations in Greece. The general default pose of anyone towards anyone else on any subject is a sort of "yeah, sure, okay," a general assumption that everyone is pretty much full of shit. Or if they've been honest, that this honesty is hiding some sort of deeper, far worse full-of-shitness. So if Eric seemed straight-up and genuine about everything so far then he was really only prepping me for this, the big crazy, or the big prank, or something. Some legitimately intensely delusional shit or some weird disgusting lie I can't even begin to figure out a reason for. Everybody lies a little about everything for no reason and here I'm supposed to treat this huge, world-altering fantasy thing better, with more trust than I would treat Carter Buehl telling me the Hummer limo he rented for prom is literally a block long?

Thing is, I don't care about Carter's block-long rape-mobile, but Eric's thing, I would love for it to be true. And I think that's part of the reason I'm pissed (because I am, among many other things, pissed right there against the wall): How dare he tell me something I want so badly to be true that so clearly isn't, and can never be?

Eric's house is quiet. He has no brothers to lead in cackling herds of friends at two in the morning on a school night, or, if they're alone, turn the TV in their room on full-volume and then get on their computer and put headphones on so they forget how on and loud the TV still is. Just the sound of two parents sleeping soundly in the same bed somewhere else upstairs, which isn't a sound at all, and the occasional creak of the house settling or whoosh of the air-conditioning coming on.

"I want you to know that it's okay if you don't believe me right away."

"Please shut up."

Books are everywhere. You could make a pretty good case for this room actually being part of a larger room and having been partitioned off by walls of books. There's a record player on the floor with three milk crates full of records next to it. A box full of disassembled action figures. Some electrical equipment I can't identify as part of one thing or another. The computer and the TV and the PlayStation. Stacks of magazines I haven't heard of. More books.

Where there is wall that you can see, including what I have my back up against, *TimeBlaze* art is tacked up. Most of it is stuff we've worked on together, but every so often there's a movie poster mocked up in Eric's really-can't-draw style. He doesn't go stick figures, the cowardly route of most people who've accepted the fact that they suck at drawing; it's just this mushy little-kid assemblage of characters with arms and legs that don't bend, just curve, big black circles for mouths, and eyes that can only convey the emotion "these shapes represent eyes." And more books.

For all that, it's not messy. My room has probably one tenth the stuff in it and is ten times as messy because everything doesn't look like it was placed where it is on purpose, just put aside without any thought before it could make its final stop in the dishwasher or the trash can or the hamper.

Eventually I have to pee. Then I really, really have to pee. I get up off the floor and tell Eric I have to go to the bathroom.

"Alright. It's down the hall on your left."

"Thanks. And let me guess: you don't ever have to pee, either." I say it a little angrier than I should if we're still friends, and I feel bad. Then I think I shouldn't feel bad, I didn't put us here, I'm not the one who said some dumb shit about not being able to sleep. But Eric laughs a little, like it's a joke. I leave and when I come back from the bathroom I am hoping to open the door and see Eric curled up on the couch with his eyes closed but he's still sitting straight up and when I come in he looks up at me, not mad or happy or anything. Not really anything but awake.

The next morning Eric and I walk to school. It has the feeling of me walking Eric to school, like I have a gun pressed to Eric's back out of sight of everyone and I'm instructing him to just act natural. Walking has the added advantage of me not having to stare directly at him: as long as he's still walking, he's not sleeping.

At school I shadow him. I am five minutes late to all my classes because after each of Eric's classes I go in and tell each one of his teachers I'm conducting research for an article in the school news-paper on stress and fatigue and Eric Lederer is my guinea pig and did you notice him sleeping in class today? All of them say no and after enough teachers telling me I picked the absolute wrong kid and Eric is always "attentive" and "polite" and "one bright little guy" I start to feel like Eric's dad at an extended parent-teacher night. Mrs. Cartwright says, "You look like you could use some *duermo* yourself, *chico.*"

In English, the class we have together, I give Eric the Cecelia Martin looking-at-a-guy-who-blew-up-a-bus stare and never waver, but he isn't anything less than one bright kid, like any other day. He never plants his elbow on the desk so his hand can hold his head somewhat upright while he dozes off mid-lecture, my per-sonal favorite sleeping-in-class position. And at lunch he's out by the loading dock as usual and I suck down a Mountain Dew, watch him, and neither of us says anything.

None of this means anything, of course. I haven't slept either, and I'm not claiming to have some superhuman ability. Today despite being unable to focus on anything in any class because I'm late to each one and can't think about anything but Eric and his made-up thing and how knocked flat I am, I try super-hard not to sleep in any classes just to prove that hey, look, I can do it too. If somebody were shadowing me around school today, they wouldn't see me close my eyes, either, though they would see me get more and more irritable and death-resembling and every so often they would see my eyelids bang together involuntarily for just a half a moment longer than a blink is, as my head dips down just slightly until I pull it back up and in my head yell at my eyelids and neck for being so fucking weak.

I come upon Eric at his locker after school and once he's done putting books away and taking books out and he zips up his back-pack we take up our formation again and walk to his house, and I am so goddamn tired. It's very hot for November first, and sweat-ing on the way home, Eric's steps next to mine an indication that he hasn't given in yet, the whole thing becomes clear to me.

Cecelia Martin and her friends pointing at Eric talking to me, quizzing me after class about our friendship: Eric and Cecelia are in cahoots. Far from enemies, they are way older friends than me and Eric. They really are friends, unlike me and Eric. She was not in English class today, so they could not pull back the curtain on their sick, ingenious, super-labor-intensive prank in front of everyone, the nerdy kid and the quasi-Goth girl revealed to be secretly in league against the kid so awkward he does not belong anywhere. It's either a very committed class project on trust or magical realism or The Picture of Dorian Gray, somehow, or just a gotcha, good for some cruel laughter. So: if he really wants to hold on until Monday, sleepless until the next time we have English, so he and Cecelia can unveil this thing to maximum effect, that's fine. I can wait. There is Mountain Dew in this world.

Settling back in on Eric's floor, I have that feeling you get when you walk into school on, say, a Wednesday: Fuck, here I am again, the same shit guaranteed by the fact that everything and everyone is obeying the same schedule and sitting in the same seats, all of us students and teachers, bored to shit. At least at school everyone's changed clothes overnight. I am in my clothes from Halloween. So is Eric. Somehow this is evidence to me.

"Why didn't you change before we went to school today?"

"Oh. I guess I didn't think of it. I have to remind myself oftentimes, and this morning I guess I had other things on my mind."

"Hmm."

"If it's alright with you I'm going to start in on my homework."

Compared to staring at an unsleeping kid every second when I want so badly to sleep myself, homework sounds kind of refreshing. But pulling out my notebook and doing Spanish freewriting right now seems like surrender somehow. Eric takes out our new English book, *Billy Budd*. Maybe he sleepwalks in a sitting position by keeping his eyes open and placing a different-colored Post-

It on every third or fourth page. It's not impossible. Nothing is impossible except that this kid doesn't sleep, is physically incapable of sleeping.

JETHRO TULL—THICK AS A BRICK—REPRISE
BRUCE SPRINGSTEEN—THE WILD, THE INNOCENT & THE E STREET SHUFFLE—COLUMBIA

My eyes are filled with words like this stacked one on top of the other. One of Eric's record crates. I am waking up on Eric's floor. I fell asleep on Eric's floor. I would like to say I had a very appropriate dream in which Eric and Cecelia Martin cut me up with kitchen knives in front of our whole English class, but I didn't, and what I did dream is disappearing fast and it had something to do with my brother and me in an empty but fully lit furniture store. It's fully lit in Eric's room, too, and with every detail of the furniture dream that evaporates I remember more of what I'm doing there, and I'm pissed at myself for falling asleep. (I almost always wake up pissed, from sleeping late, or not sleeping enough, and if you don't always wake up pissed I think you're living wrong.) I sit up and Eric is on the couch, awake, pages from the end of *Billy Budd*, it looks like. A piece of data that means nothing since I haven't been consistently awake to watch Eric be the same, he could've just flipped to the end of the book after a nap just a little shorter than mine.

There is also now a video camera on a tripod standing at one end of the couch, pointing at Eric, with its screen flipped to face him as well.

Eric notices me. "I taped myself," he says, "so you can see."

"What time is it?"

Eric holds up his digital alarm clock. It reads 11:00 p.m.

"I started right after you fell asleep," Eric says. "Would you like to see it?"

Before I can respond, Eric gets up, stops the camera recording, and hits Rewind. The tape whirs while Eric goes to his closet, which is just as full of stuff as his room, and gets out a cord he uses to connect the camera to his TV. The tape finishes rewinding. Eric hits Play.

On TV, colorful magnetic fridge letters dance on a carpet, spelling out *Cannibal Island 3: The Reckoning.*

"I completely forgot this was on here," Eric says. "For a while I was really into stop-motion animation." Eric hits Fast Forward and a little movie about Lego men on an island of mutants speeds by. I recognize a lot of the shattered action figures from the bin in the corner and I see how they got that way. (Stop-motion harpoons, stop-motion torpedoes, a stop-motion fall from a plateau that is probably also Eric's kitchen table.) Then, super-fast, some credits in magnetic fridge letters then two seconds of black during which Eric hits Play, then on-screen this afternoon's Eric is looking down the camera's barrel, holding up the clock, which reads 4:30 p.m. Then he pans left to reveal me, curled up on the floor, eyes closed. Then he pans back, checks to make sure the angle's okay, then carefully places the clock in the frame, sits down, and picks up *Billy Budd.* Eric on camera looks up, then readjusts the way he's holding the book so the camera can see his open unsleeping eyes better. In real life, Eric hits Fast Forward again, and on screen, the clock starts advancing one minute per second or more and in the bedroom window behind Eric's head the light starts changing, sharp white daylight to orange to purple as the sun sets. It's almost totally dark when Eric's head dips and his eyes close.

"Wait!" I say. "What's—stop the tape."

Eric hits Play. On TV, tears leak out of his closed eyes. His head turns away from the camera. He gets up, leaves frame, the bedroom light comes on, Eric returns, sits down again. The crying is over but his eyes are still red.

Eric hits Fast Forward and the final three hours of dark speed by and the clock gets closer to the time it is now. I think about editing tricks, stop motion. I vaguely think of Cecelia, but she is getting harder and harder to work into the equation. On-screen, Eric speaks to someone off-screen, me waking up five minutes ago. The tape ends.

"Good thing you woke up when you did," Eric says, "or I would have had to switch tapes."

For a second I let myself live in a world where what Eric's said is the truth, where all the evidence that it's true isn't a pack of lies to be debunked. In this world my betrayal and confusion about how to feel about this kid is replaced with relief, and my heart swells and my brain practically explodes out of the front of my head at the idea that this is actually happening to me. Then I put one mental foot back in the mundane world of Eric being crazy or a liar or both, where we say "yeah, sure, okay" even in response to the smallest stuff it's easy and low-stakes to believe. I go back and forth, feeling my heart get either huge and kid-like or small and full of poison.

"You didn't have coffee, or anything?" I say to Eric.

Eric says: "Are we talking now?"

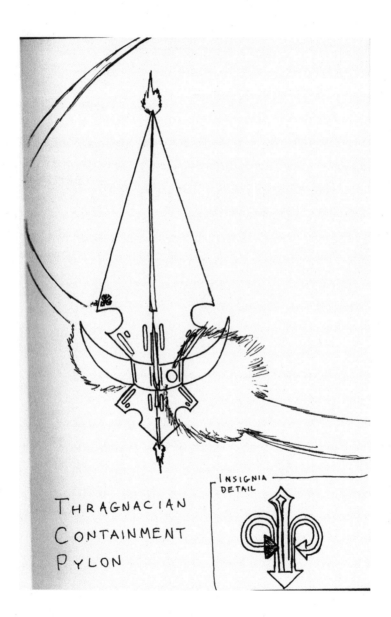

THRAGNACIAN
CONTAINMENT
PYLON

INSIGNIA
DETAIL

4

"Who else have you told? You said you've said it before three or four times."

"Both my parents. You. Cecelia Martin."

"You told *Cecelia Martin?*"

"I thought she was cool. I thought she would understand."

"Really? What gave you that impression?"

"We like the same things. Or at least I thought we did."

"That's, like, a pretty lame reason to tell somebody this."

"I know. I fully realize. But in the past year or so I've gotten really aggressively tired of nobody knowing. I tried to evaluate who might be a good person to tell, and I realized there was no one immediately close to me, so I guess I didn't do a very good job."

"Can I be honest with you? Before I decided to believe you, I was pretty much convinced that this was like, some practical joke you and Cecelia were playing on me."

"Why would you think that?"

"Her and her friends are sort of fixated on you. And I thought maybe it was that they were fixated on you talking to me, because you were working on selling me on this prank, looking at you like 'what a good job he's doing, how hilarious is this?' You know?"

"Well, it's not that. She thinks I'm crazy and has probably told everyone she encounters just that."

"She told me that. I guess I thought it was all part of your big plan, or something. I don't know. I was really tired and this is . . . a lot."

"Thank you for believing me. You are now officially the only person who knows."

"But your parents know?"

"Just because I told them doesn't mean they believed it."

"When did you tell them?"

"When I was ten."

"I thought you said it's been like this your whole life."

"It has been, but I never realized I was different. As a baby I probably just lay there awake, but once I got old enough to understand that other people slept, and that every night I was in bed just like everybody else, I guess I figured I was sleeping. I guess I thought lying in bed with your eyes closed was what everybody did. I didn't realize your state was supposed to change, or that people actually shut off. I guess I just thought it was a really boring eight hours everybody had to go through, lying there awake and calling it sleep. A ritual or something."

"So you just laid there for your whole childhood?"

"Yeah. It got boring after a while. After I learned to read, once my parents were asleep and they thought I was asleep, I would get up and go get a book. I felt guilty, like if you were in church and you were supposed to be praying but instead you were thinking about girls or something. I didn't think anything was wrong with me, I just thought maybe I was a bad kid who didn't dutifully lie there. But it was too boring to keep doing it like I thought you were supposed to."

"But dreams . . . You must've seen people in movies or cartoons or whatever have dreams and thought, 'I don't have those.' "

"I thought I did. I guess they were just daydreams. But incredibly vivid ones. You know that subconscious thing you were talking about? I think my mind just processes those things all the time behind the scenes. My imagination is something of a badass."

It is weird and kind of funny to hear Eric say "badass." I am used to describing some *TimeBlaze* character or vehicle as "badass" before he goes to write its dossier, and him asking me if I can't be more specific.

"So how did you figure it out?"

"A cartoon, like you said. Donald Duck is trying to get to sleep and water keeps dripping out of the faucet and waking him up. He gets progressively angrier."

"Oh yeah, I've seen that one."

"Right. And I didn't understand why he was so upset. I thought, if I were him, I'd be happy for the distraction. I wouldn't want to go back to bed and just lie there. It wasn't an instant thing. I didn't say 'Eureka.' But that was the first time I thought something might be off about me."

"And you told your parents?"

"Yes. They took it to mean I was having trouble sleeping. I was trying to articulate it to them, but if something's been a certain way your entire life, it's difficult to make someone understand how it's weird, when you yourself just started to realize that it's weird."

"So they just gave you warm milk and whatever." My mom used to give me warm milk when I was a kid and couldn't sleep. I slept easier nights afterward just wanting to avoid drinking warm milk, which is the strangest thing your mouth can experience, being used to cold milk in cereal and in a glass beside every meal growing up. It's like seeing your teacher outside of school. It's them, but they're all wrong and out of context.

"Warm milk, yes. And Children's Tylenol PM. So I would just lie there . . . you know . . . stoned."

I laugh. Eric laughs.

"I told them. I kept telling them. My mom told me that if it was really bothering me, we could go to a sleep specialist. So I stopped telling them."

"You've never been to a doctor for it?"

"No. Not a chance. If they found out . . ."

"Who's THEY?"

Eric looks at me like, you oughta know.

"If they found out, what? Man, you were a paranoid ten-year-old."

"I'd seen *E.T.*"

"Yeah, I gotcha." Somewhere we picked up the unspoken idea that if there's something unique about you, men in suits and dark glasses will show up to take you away. Something about it felt scary and right, like yes, that is exactly what goes down when you're special.

"So what do you think it is?"

"You mean what do I think caused it?"

"Yeah."

"I don't know. A mutation or radiation exposure or a new stage in human evolution."

"Yeah, that's what I would say, except . . ."

"None of those things are real."

"Right."

"Right, well . . . here I am."

"Do you ever get tired?"

"I guess. I mean, there are times I feel tired, but from what I understand, people who have to sleep feel tired sometimes and it has nothing to do with whether or not they've gotten enough sleep."

That's true. Every day I tell myself I'm not going to fall asleep in geometry, and no matter how much sleep I've gotten the night before I still end up nodding off with my head propped up on my hand.

"If I experience fatigue, I just feel it for a while and before long I feel better."

"What do you do with all that time? I mean, when everybody else is asleep?"

"I get interested in things. I might get really interested in jazz music and just want to learn everything about jazz, so I do. I get my homework done fast. I get projects done a week in advance so I have time for other things. It's like . . . this is . . . I've thought this but I've never said it out loud before, but it's like, there's me and there's everyone else in the world, and everyone else is in a constant state of joining me and leaving me. When they leave, it's sort of lonely, I suppose, but I have time to think and do things uninterrupted. I go for walks."

I guess that's how my brother and his friends found him that night. I guess that's how he knew the ins and outs of that street all the way across town when my brother and his friends found us on Halloween, getting flimsy and unoriginal revenge.

"I'm sorry I didn't just . . ." I say. "I'm sorry, I just had to see for myself that you don't . . . you know."

"It's okay. I understand. Even that, even waiting around to find out, was a kind of believing, I think. More than anybody else has ever done, anyway. While you were, I guess, thinking about how Cecelia and I were getting one over on you, I was thinking that. That the fact that you didn't just immediately say, 'Screw off, Eric,' that was as close to complete and immediate trust as something as wild as this deserves."

I think of Eric in that one moment between fast-forwards, crying it looked like. Even if he says it's okay I still feel like pretty much of an asshole, following a stone miracle around for thirty-six hours going, "Prove it!"

We sit there talking about it for hours. Even with the unintentional nap, I expected to feel tired at some point. I thought I might need coffee or soda or something. But I guess your best friend telling you he can't sleep and then finally deciding you believe him has the same effect as not needing to sleep and not being able to, at least for a little while.

Eventually, the sun has risen. I can hear Eric's parents rustling around downstairs.

At some point I tell him I should go home. I am never away from home for this long consecutively, and before Eric, I was barely away from home at all, but because of my brother being my brother, I know how long my dad can stand one of his offspring not being around and not checking in at all. It's not when anyone normal's parents start to worry, it's more a time about twelve hours after normal people's parents start to worry that my dad realizes he isn't worried and that's what starts to worry him.

"When was the last time you saw your brother?" he'll ask me.

"Tuesday night."

And I think in his head he starts up an imaginary conversation with a custody judge or my mom or the cop who comes by to tell him they found my brother floating in the canal after not quite being able to jump it with his car, and realizes that for the sake of looking not-so-bad in that imaginary future conversation he should probably start to worry, or go through the phone-dialing motions worried people go through, though he knows we're okay.

Phones are like these talismans for me and my brother and my dad. Like, as long as we have our phones on us, my brother and I, there is no way we could be hurt or kidnapped or impaled on anything. The one or two times I've been out of the house and needed to call and let him know I'd be out the house longer have gone like this:

"Hey, Dad?"

"Hello?"

"Hey, I'll be late tonight."

"Okay. Got your phone on you?"

"Yep."

"Alright. Be safe."

"Bye."

"Bye."

We have the same kind of phone and we're all on the same phone plan. I know full well that when I call him from my phone my name shows up, indicating that I'm calling from my phone, and that in order to be doing that, I must have my phone on me. It's so dumb I think with any other kind of dad it would be a dad joke. But my dad doesn't joke so much as he goes to the gym all the time.

I get up off the floor of Eric's room. "It was nice having someone to stay up with," he says.

When I get home at ten or so on Saturday morning my brother's car isn't there. It's probably wrapped around a pole or he got arrested for lighting trash cans on fire and rolling them into traffic last night or he's at the morning youth mass with Cathy and Alan and Tits, who's Jewish but goes because of peer pressure. I go to my room and lock the door and fall asleep on top of my sheets with my clothes on and when I wake up it's dark outside and I have one of those weird is-it-morning-what-day-is-it half-awake slept-the-day-away feelings, and I remember what Eric told me. I try to think whether it was a dream or not, and then I remember that it wasn't, and I think that Eric's been awake this whole day while I've been asleep, and Eric's been awake since I've known him, and Eric's been awake since he was born.

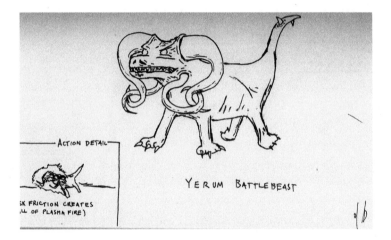

ACTION DETAIL

...SK FRICTION CREATES
...LL OF PLASMA FIRE)

YERUM BATTLEBEAST

5

Eric always insists that our characters have a weakness. The Thragnacian hell-beast has a soft and glowing underbelly which Martian
Praetoreous can hit with his arm-mounted crossbow. Being cybernetic, the AltraTroops are susceptible to biohacking, an arcane art
practiced by the laptop monks who dwell in The Spoke, an aborted
half-constructed space platform. The Man is the only character without a weakness. He is holographic and infinitely self-replicating. No
one knows where he is or what he is or if he's even human and you
can't kill him because it's very possible there's nothing there to kill.

I live in a world where what Eric told me is true. And it isn't always
an easy thing to fit into your head but it almost helps that Cecelia

Martin didn't believe him. Cecelia Martin has exactly zero imagination. It's not that Cecelia Martin is dumb, it's just that she's so
fucking standard and convinced that she isn't because her hair is
dyed a different color and she listens to music that she finds on
LiveJournals that mostly feature pictures of emo boys making out
with each other. I think I understand why Eric told her. If this were
a movie she'd be the person you'd go to. The freaky chick, the outcast. But Cecelia Martin is on yearbook and newspaper. Cecelia
Martin gets straight A's. Cecelia Martin is about as outcast as the
head fucking cheerleader. I want to believe where she had the
chance to and didn't because it doesn't fit in with Cecelia Martin's
worldview, which pretty much begins with Cecelia Martin and her
friends Jen Ackerman and Teresa Saylor and whatever cute vintage
finds they've made this week, and their college friends and how
sophisticated and ironic they are.

I can imagine it: Eric hears Cecelia use the words *temporal* and
agonize in some in-class discussion. Eric suspects that Cecelia
may, in fact, be smart. That night at home Eric looks up Cecelia's
Namespot profile, Namespot being the social networking site on
which millions of American kids advertise their specialness,
despite the fact that there is a search-engine tool right there on the
sidebar that will allow you to find out just how hugely unspecial
you are. Eric sees that under "Music" Cecelia has expressed a pref-
erence for The Boy Who Cried Sparrow, a pretty okay and sort of
obscure group people found out about from their older siblings
who are in college, which Eric, underexposed as he is to anybody,
ever, doesn't realize is a thing anyone else is into, takes it to be a
sign, and without hesitation camps out waiting for Cecelia outside
of English class the next day and, unbidden, stutters at her something about he has a secret only she can understand, and before
she can even ask "What?" he blurts it out, all nervous and half-
intelligible, so that now when she asks "What?" it isn't because she
wants to know the secret, it's because he already said the secret
and she couldn't understand him. So he says it again, too loud this
time, overcompensating, and she probably says something very

close to what I said initially, something like "Oh, so don't drink so much caffeine or whatever," and starts to walk away, supremely weirded out, when Eric stops her and tries ultra-awkwardly to explain, but he has no idea where to start and this isn't going at all like he planned it, and she stops him four half-sentences into his explanation and says, "I seriously have no idea what you're talking about. I have to get to class." One of the four half-sentences had something to do with how they both liked the same music, and so now she goes around telling anyone who will listen that Eric Lederer, you know, that weird kid, well, he basically stalked her and said some crazy stuff she doesn't even know how to repeat and he ought to be red-flagged like Carl Whiteman, he probably has a hit list and everything, she's probably on it, enjoy her while she's here, alive, and hasn't yet been murdered by the stalker nerd.

And that day, I probably walked right by them out of class, not really knowing either of them or having any idea who they'd end up being to me, but I can imagine it so accurately because I was then (and I guess I am still) in my own world of misreading people, reaching out to them in an awkward, overplanned way that blows up big-time, then retreating back in to my just-me existence, while they go around telling anyone who will listen what a tard I am.

Eric's thing, I don't know what to call it, sounds like something Eric and I would have made up. And I guess I want to live in a world where things like Eric can exist.

And for a while that in itself is exciting. If Eric can exist despite the fact that Eric existing is impossible, then other things that are impossible can happen. They're out there living among us and we have no idea. I spend an entire day thinking about this. The gray-haired cashier at Safeway, he can sense people's intentions and disarm robbers before they try anything, which is why the store has never been robbed. Shoplifters he lets through because they're not worth blowing his cover, which is why my brother has never been caught at that particular store. The Mexican housekeepers waiting for the shuttle bus on what shouldn't be a hot day because it's November but it is, they house the reincarnated souls of Aztec warlords and if they got close enough to a certain temple in South America they'd become thirty-foot-tall fire-beasts instead of gossipy old women.

But then on the way into school I see Brendan Tyler, a varsity basketball player, standing in front of the black sports car his parents got him when he crashed his last car, arms folded. A bunch of people are gathered around. "I'd give my left nut for that car," a kid says. Brendan reaches in the front window and tweaks a knob that makes his car stereo's bass rattle, shaking the windows of the cars around him. I think, if anybody else had what Eric had, they'd probably show it off every chance they got. There would be no secret. They'd be in the school parking lot using their mysterious God-given mutation to make hot girls more receptive to fingerbanging. Eric's probably the only one of his kind, which makes him all the more important to protect. Protect, if that's what I'm doing by being his friend and keeping his secret. For some reason *protect* is the word that comes to mind.

"This isn't going to change anything, is it?" Eric says when I see him for the first time Monday at lunch. "My thing?"

And that's what we end up calling it. "Eric's thing." Not "Eric's mutation" or "Eric's evolutionary leap" or "Eric's freak ability." Although if I had my way we'd call it all those things and get to the bottom of what it is without tipping off anyone who might want to use it for evil and in the meantime use it for good, all while nobody has any idea and keeps on thinking we're two kids who don't talk to anybody and don't eat in the lunchroom, all while everybody keeps on not knowing we exist at all.

"No," I say, "it doesn't have to." But it's pretty hard to keep drawing time travelers and biomodified quasi-humans when the real fucking thing is sitting next to you, eating pretzel sticks and whistling a Brazilian jazz tune. Eric's really into Brazil this week.

On Monday night my brother finds me in my room doing my

homework. Apparently he has not forgotten that four nights ago my friend and I tried to egg his friend's house and made him run to chase us when he'd really rather not because he smokes half a pack a day and probably interrupted his best friend getting some from his girlfriend or whatever girl that was, and worst of all, got away so he didn't get instant release right at the moment when he was at his angriest. And now he has to work hard to get angry again and that's a pain so he takes that out on me, too. I barely feel it as he whales on me. He has no idea. Nobody does. My friend is a Greek god. My friend is an alien. My friend and I are the only people in the world who know that the world is not as simple and boring as everybody thinks it is and my friend is the only piece of evidence that that is true. I hit back a little so I don't come off totally weird, but my brother works out and I don't and it has no effect. It doesn't matter. The joke is on him and Cecelia Martin and the rest of the world, and I would laugh if that wouldn't come off totally weird in the middle of all the punching.

"So I've been pricing screenwriting software, and it's pretty expensive, but once we sell the *TimeBlaze* franchise we'll be—"

"Have you ever gone to the dentist?"

"What?"

"The dentist."

"Yes, of course I've been to the dentist. Is this some subtle way of telling me to brush more often?"

"My brother had his wisdom teeth out a couple years ago, and they put him under. Like, gas."

"Okay."

"Do you think that would work on you? Do you think you'd go under?"

"I really have no idea. Do you remember what I told you about Children's Tylenol PM when I was a kid?"

"Yeah."

"I imagine it would have the same effect."

"That's Children's Tylenol PM versus industrial-strength anesthesia. That's like a bowie knife versus the A-bomb. If that doesn't knock you out . . ."

"That's assuming I want to be 'knocked out.' "

"Don't you?"

Eric doesn't say anything. It's lunchtime on Tuesday, the day after my brother whaled on me for the Halloween incident. We are out by the loading dock. My Styrofoam soda cup is full of teeth marks and Eric's lunch is as elaborate as ever.

"Well anyway, it's not about wanting to get knocked out, it's about testing the limits of your power!"

"Can we please not call it a 'power'? It's not a 'power'! I'm not enabled to do anything spectacular. There's just something I can't do."

"It's all how you think of it. It's, like, either you can't sleep, which implies that you would if you could, or you don't HAVE to sleep, you have the power of never sleeping—"

"Can we just NOT call it a power? It's just . . . a thing."

"Okay, a thing."

Eric starts nesting his Tupperware containers, one inside another, and then puts the whole thing in his backpack like he does every day.

"All I'm saying is, if your teeth start hurting, it might be your wisdom teeth coming in, and that might be a good opportunity to test the limits of your . . . thing."

"I'll be sure and let you know," Eric says.

We go over to Eric's house after school instead of my house so Eric doesn't get the same treatment from my brother that I got. We are roughing out a gang of zombie outlaws that pursue Cowboy Praetoreous across the night-deserts of Hell County. Eric is writing their bios and stats on the back of profile pictures I've drawn.

"I like that he still has the noose around his neck," Eric says, "and there's a bite taken out of his shin." *He was bit by the gang as he kicked on the hangin' tree,* Eric writes on the back. For each different timestream, the bios are in a different voice, or if not that, a different style of lettering.

"So your body is constantly regenerating itself without the aid of sleep," I say. "What does that feel like?"

"It doesn't feel like anything," Eric says, "or at least not anything I would notice as out of the ordinary."

"Oh," I say.

His parents invite me to stay for dinner. They are normal and boring. Nothing about them says they'd given birth to the next stage in human evolution. Eric's dad looks nerdy like Eric. Eric's mom looks like she could be an English teacher. They both work in computers. They're not divorced, and I guess that's unusual enough for this neighborhood that maybe there is something mutated in their genes. They ask me about my dad and my brother and how school is going. Dinner is less fancy than the stuff Eric makes for himself.

"Can Darren stay over tonight?" Eric asks. He hasn't asked me if I want to, but he knows my dad won't care and he knows I'd rather not go home until my brother has forgotten about being mad at me and has instead started being mad at the booker at the Pisscutter for not booking enough real hardcore bands or mad at Cathy for cigarette-burning the roof of his car near the dome light, both things he has been very mad about before.

Eric's mom says it's fine with them if it's okay with my dad and I stand up from the table and go to another room, take out my cell phone, and have the following conversation:

"Hey, Dad?"

"Hello?"

"Hey, I'm gonna stay over at Eric's tonight."

"Okay. Got your phone on you?"

"Yep."

"Alright. Be safe."

"Bye."

"Bye."

I go into the kitchen, where Eric's parents are doing the dishes, and when I say "Thank you, Mrs. Lederer," she doesn't say, "Call me ————," her first name, like parents of your friends sometimes do.

"He looks normal up-front," Eric says, "but his back is full of holes," referring to a zombie outlaw who in life was betrayed by a member of his gang. "Now, resurrected, he always sits facing the door."

"Space dust," I say, "or cosmic rays. I mean, I know those things sound comic-booky, but honestly, ANYTHING could be possible."

"Can we not talk about it anymore?" Eric says. "Let's just focus on the project."

"Sorry," I say. "It's just a lot more interesting than anything we've come up with—"

"You don't like what we come up with?"

"It's not that, it's just this thing is REAL. I mean, you really wanted me to believe you, and I do, but part of me believing it is, I don't know, it's something you've known all your life or almost all of it so it doesn't bother you, but me, Jesus, I just got used to life not being everything you think it's going to be or might be when you're a kid, and your thing kind of makes it seem like maybe that's not true, like maybe stuff like this is possible, I mean, it's not possible, but here it is anyway."

"I guess I can't blame you for being curious," Eric says, "but if your friend couldn't walk, everything you asked them wouldn't be about how they couldn't walk. The fact that they couldn't walk wouldn't be the sole focus of your friendship."

"No, but if you just found out they couldn't walk," I say, "and besides, that comparison doesn't even make sense, everybody wants to be able to walk, walking makes life easier, but I'll bet you if you gave them the option there are tons of people who'd say they'd never sleep if they didn't have to. I probably wouldn't. Sleep is terrible. It's like, you have to do it, your body forces you to, makes you want to. I mean, sometimes you dream, sometimes it actually feels like time is passing but you never really get to enjoy being asleep. Mostly it's just like fast-forwarding to the next day. You go to school and come home and do your homework and by that time you're tired and you go to sleep and you wake up and you have to go to school again. And if you do stay up to put off having to go to school the next day, when you DO have to go to school you're exhausted and it's even worse than it would've been otherwise. It robs you of all this time. Which I guess means you've had all that time. I guess . . . I guess that means you're like twice as old as any of us."

"How do you mean?"

"You've been awake while the rest of us have been asleep. You've actually had more life, in terms of being awake and aware of things. So you're twice as old, in terms of experience. You're like thirty."

"I believe the average human being spends a third of their life sleeping, so technically I'm about twenty."

"But still! There's something about you that's like, this kid is not like other kids, this kid is older, this kid knows something we don't."

"You wouldn't think that if you didn't know about my thing. You're only saying that because you want to see me as different because now you know I'm different."

"Nuh-uh! No, man, the first day when you stood in front of my desk and you wanted to know what I was drawing, I noticed there was something about the way you stood, like, you didn't shift from foot to foot or anything like people usually do when they take the chance of getting up out of their seat and crossing the room and talking to somebody, and having to stand up in front of somebody and put yourself on the line, any time I've ever done something like that I get all weird and fidgety."

"I wasn't asking you out, I just wanted to know what you were drawing."

"Regardless, dude, I noticed something different."

And it's true, I did. Those drawing books that don't help, something they always tell you to do is observe people in real life. The way they stand, the "line" of their posture, so you can break it down into lines and basketballs and potato sacks and whatever. So I notice when somebody has their feet planted, when they're standing straight up, as opposed to slouching or moving around like they're nervous. Not that it helps. I have a hard time drawing anybody not standing straight up with their arms at their sides. I don't stand as straight as the people I draw. Not at all.

"Anyway, I'm sorry, you're probably sorry you told me about it now," I say. "It's just that if I had what you have I think I'd be more excited about it."

"You wouldn't."

I think for a second about how it's weird that I've been drawing on the floor in Eric's room, papers spread around me, propped up on my elbows, whatever page I'm drawing on placed on top of a comic-book trade paperback. It makes me feel really young.

"I'm not sorry I told you," Eric says. "It's nice being up with someone to talk to."

"I can lay off if you want," I say.

Eric shrugs. It's four in the morning. I yawn.

"Do you want to go to sleep?" Eric says.

I don't. "You know what it must be like?" I say. "Crossfire."

"Like our character?" Eric says. We have a character named Crossfire. Every part of him is a gun.

"No, there was this game when we were kids, Crossfire. A board game. It had awesome commercials, it looked awesome. Like two of my friends in first grade had it, and whenever I'd go over to their houses I'd want to play it, but they would never want to. They had Crossfire, they knew it wasn't as awesome as the commercials made it look. And you know what? It did suck. But it seemed cool to me because I didn't have it, so I didn't know."

"It doesn't suck," Eric says, "not completely." He smiles. "Not as much as Crossfire."

On one of his night walks, Eric found a Super Nintendo on the sidewalk with a bunch of things people were throwing out. We play old-school games until it's really totally morning.

I realize I'm going to be wearing the same clothes at school today that I wore yesterday. Eric offers to let me borrow one of his shirts, but they're all the kind of short-sleeved polo shirts he always wears that I would never wear, so I say I'm okay. I wear this black T-shirt pretty much every day anyway, and these same jeans, and either way I doubt anyone will notice. We put on our backpacks. School is within walking distance of Eric's house.

Walking to school I have that weird euphoric giddiness you get from being up all night. It's sunny, of course, but it's the first cool day this year, it's the desert version of "crisp," like 70 degrees, but noticeably different. It might be 90 again by lunch but for now it's cool. I will crash by third period but for now everything is beautiful. I wonder if Eric ever gets like this or if it's all pretty much the same, since he never has to get sleep he never gets giddy from the lack of it. I don't ask, though. We stop at the gas station around the corner from school to get Mountain Dew and something to eat for breakfast.

Our routine goes pretty much like this: I go over to Eric's house after school or Eric comes over to my house after school. If Eric is over at my house he calls his parents to see if it's cool if he stays for dinner, except there's really no dinner to stay for a lot of times, it's just whatever dinner we can scrounge up or whatever my dad orders in. Occasionally he barbecues something or we go out to eat and we bring Eric along and Eric stares in awe as my dad and my brother swear at each other playfully in the middle of Outback Steakhouse. Sometimes when my dad's not around Eric cooks whatever we have in the kitchen, so he's gotten pretty creative with eggs and frozen steaks and five-pound freezer bags of stir-fry vegetables from Costco.

If I'm over at Eric's house I don't have to call but sometimes I do

anyway right in front of Eric's parents so they don't think I'm some
child of neglect or something. If I'm going over to Eric's I'll stop
off home and put my Xbox in my backpack. There's enough room
for it and two controllers if I take all my school stuff out. It comes
in handy when Eric and I are tired of making stuff and want to use
somebody else's characters to kick the ever-living shit out of each
other for a while.

I start to crash at around four or five in the morning, especially
if it's a school night. Eric and I will shoot the shit for a while before
I fall asleep, on the nights that I do fall asleep. Sometimes I stay
awake the whole time despite Eric telling me it's cool and I can
sleep whenever I want to. It's sort of like being at a restaurant with
somebody and you're hungry and they're not and they tell you it's
fine, go ahead and order, so you do and when the food comes no
matter how many times they tell you they're really not hungry, they
couldn't eat a thing, you can't help but feel awkward about eating.
It was like this with my mom once at a Perkins when she visited,
and it's how it is with me and Eric and sleep.

Most of the time I sleep right through my weekend days. I get
home around nine or ten in the morning, or Eric leaves around
then if he's been over, and I spend the whole day in bed with the
TV on drifting in and out of naps, half-following whatever it is I'm
watching. One Sunday I have TBS on and I'm half-asleep. Some
mob movie is on. The same five or six actors that are always in
mob movies are in this movie, and at the moment, three or four
guys have one guy down on his knees caught in the headlights of
this car they've got parked out in the middle of nowhere. I gather
the guy on his knees was a crooked cop and people started to catch
on to him so he squealed and sold out the mob guys he was
crooked for and they're not too happy. One of the goons goes into
the trunk and pulls out a bat, and in my almost-dreaming way I get
an idea I think I should tell Eric about. I resolve to get up and go
tell Eric about it but instead I close my eyes and fall asleep for
another hour or two. I wake up around three and the movie is over
but I remember the idea so I get up, take a shower, pull on some

clothes, and take the bus over to Eric's. My whole reasoning for the idea or why I thought it was so great is gone with whatever half-dream I was half-having involving mobsters and probably sex and probably my mom or something equally dream-fucked, but the idea is still there and the resolve to tell Eric and the conviction that for some reason it's a great idea.

I'm going to tell Eric that I think if we knock him out, like physically knock him out, maybe that will work. Maybe that's worth a try, in place of waiting for his wisdom teeth to come in, as a way to test his susceptibility to unconsciousness. My hair is dry by the time I get off the bus near Eric's street.

Eric's mom answers the door.

"Hi, Mrs. Lederer." I still haven't been invited to call her whatever her first name is. She lets me in and tells me Eric's upstairs and hasn't been down all day.

There's a strong possibility, I think, that both of us were lying around in our underwear watching TV all day on opposite sides of town, except one of us was falling in and out of sleep and the other one had his eyes open the whole time with nothing to succumb to when the show he was watching got boring. I go upstairs and knock on Eric's door.

"Go away," comes Eric's voice from inside.

"Dude, it's me."

"GO AWAY."

"What's wrong?"

Nothing for a second, then the sound of the door unlocking. Eric just barely opens the door and sticks his head out of the crack. He looks like an absolute nightmare: his eyes are bloodshot, there are dark circles under them, he looks like he's sweating out malaria or something.

"Just trust me, okay? You have to go. Don't tell my mom. I'll see you later. I'll be fine. Just go."

"Dude, what's going—"

All of the sudden Eric yelps and turns to look into the room like someone's coming at him and I can't see in the room well enough to know what's going on but it doesn't sound like there's anybody in there and Eric pulls his head back in and screams and slams the door shut all in one motion like he's trying to keep something from getting out, but like I said, I don't hear anything or anybody except for his breathing, heavy on the other side of the door. Just like he asked me to, I go downstairs. His mom is standing at the bottom of the stairs and asks me if everything's alright in a way that indicates she suspects that not everything is alright.

"Yes. It is," I say, just like Eric asked me to, and although he didn't ask me to lie in such an unconvincing way, I'm doing my best here. I walk calmly to the front door and see myself out.

I'd think maybe Eric has a drug problem if I didn't spend all my time with him and know for a fact that he'd have no idea where to get heroin, and that he's never expressed interest in anything besides the thousand little nerdy corners of things he gets interested in for a week at a time before discarding and maybe, MAYBE the slightest interest in girls, and even then not really girls but more the idea of girls. I'd think maybe Eric has some tropical disease if I didn't know for a fact he hasn't been to any third-world jungles recently.

I wait for the bus for a little while. I wait but as I'm waiting I think, "It'll be faster just to walk," and even though I know that isn't true by that time I'm already committed to walking.

Eric calls me that night. My phone vibrates on the edge of my nightstand. My dad pointed out one time that my minute use makes up only 1 percent of our "family plan" bill, and he and my brother had a good laugh about that, but one month when my brother sent more than five thousand text messages we both got our phones taken away.

"Hey, man."

"Hi. I'm sorry about earlier."

"Yeah, what the fuck?"

"It's another thing with . . . the thing." For somebody who usually throws around so many words, when Eric talks about his "thing" he gets extremely vague. "Every couple of weeks, I'll have a twenty-four hour-period where . . . I don't know. Essentially it's miserable. I start hallucinating. These extremely vivid hallucinations. I get headaches. I sort of have to lock myself away and there's nothing to do until it passes."

You can't sleep it off, I almost say but don't. "Jesus, dude. You never told me about this."

"Yes, I don't know, I guess . . . I know it's troublesome. I've never seen myself from the outside, I guess. Was it bad?"

"You looked really bad."

"Jeez, I'm sorry, I guess I should've warned you about it before . . ."

"How does your mom not know? Or your dad?"

"I just shut myself in my room. I just shut myself in my room and they don't really bother me."

I think about the way I spent all day, and think that I guess it's not that implausible for a teenage boy to spend the whole day in his room, with nobody bothering him and no reason for them to, especially on a weekend.

Monday at lunch I'm Eric, which means I'm the one who's spent all weekend obsessing over something, and I'm the one with diagrams and charts and pitches and ideas. Well, I don't really have diagrams or charts or anything written down, even. But I have been thinking about this one thing a lot and I can't wait to talk about it.

"So this thing this weekend," I say.

At first I was mad at Eric for not telling me about these fits when he told me about his not-sleeping thing. And I'm mad at him for not letting us talk about or even name his "thing," beyond it being just a "thing." Remaining nameless makes it harder to talk about, which is probably what he wants. But either way, it is a part of his thing. It makes it more real and it means that whatever we

call it, or don't call it, it might go beyond just Eric lacking the ability to sleep. And of course it does, and I always sort of knew it did,
but we can't really explore it unless he lets us, and he hasn't.

"I have a theory about it," I say. "When you sleep, your body
works out shit in your subconscious. That's what dreams are. But
you don't sleep so you never have a chance to work any of that stuff
out. So it just builds up and builds up and it comes out when
you're awake. Which is always. But in these, like, superconcen-
trated bursts."

A second goes by. I'm waiting for Eric to say it's genius. Instead
he says, "Yeah, I know."

"You know? Know what?"

"I know what they are. I've had them my whole life."

"Well first of all, you don't know what they are, you don't know
anything about this or where it comes from or what causes it,
you said so. So you don't 'know' it any more than I do, and I've
just . . . like I said, it's a theory. And the other thing is, you pretend
like you don't think about this, your secret, but that's bullshit, you
think about everything, you obsess over details, and this has to be
the biggest most interesting thing in your life, and you're telling
me you don't think about it? Of course you think about it. Like, you
already 'know' why you've had these hallucinations, you've thought
about it, so quit acting like . . ."

"Acting like what?" Eric says.

"Like this isn't important. Or I guess stop acting like it isn't
amazing. Just fucking admit to the fact that you're special."

"I told you," Eric says, "people can't find out because . . ."

"I know!" I say. "They'll cart you away and hook you up to
machines and whatever. I'm not saying you have to put it in the
school newspaper."

"Okay I'm special," Eric says.

"If we let it this could be an adventure," I say.

"I don't see how," Eric says.

"Somebody finds out they have special abilities, and then the
adventure begins."

We both grew up on comic books and *Star Wars*. I just can't understand how he wouldn't be high all the time off the fact that he might be the chosen one.

Eric's elaborate self-made lunches come with their own brought-from-home silverware. He's scraping the tines of his fork on the concrete in the shadowy corner of the loading dock.

"Sorry if it scared you," Eric says. "And thank you for not telling anybody."

"Don't worry about it."

"If you want. If you want, we could look into . . . what it takes for me to not be conscious."

"Serious?"

"Yes."

"Okay. Friday after school."

It's quiet and then the bell rings.

"Well, we're NOT hitting me over the head with a bat. We just aren't."

"No, right, of course. It wasn't an 'idea' per se. Just more of, like, a concept."

Eric and I are walking home after school on Friday. Other kids' cars speed by on the main road that runs past our school. The Drama Club has put flyers for their upcoming production underneath everybody's windshield wipers and nobody's taking them out, just driving away and letting them fly off on their own, so the street is a mess of Day-Glo-orange paper. Brendan Tyler's new car, the one I overheard some idiot saying he'd give his left nut to have, accelerates to pass some band girl in a Camry. I am certain I would rather have both testicles than that car, even if it means I have to walk everywhere.

"So the mob method is out. Your wisdom teeth aren't coming in? Like at all?"

Eric runs his tongue around his mouth for effect. "No."

"Okay. Well, I still don't think Children's Tylenol PM is a very good measure of how narcotics affect your thing."

"Narcotics? I'm not sure I'm all that excited about where this seems to be heading."

"Relax. I don't mean like, black tar heroin. There are lots of substances that are legal and safe that we can get our hands on."

I don't see my brother's car speeding by, and I wonder if that means he's home already.

"It's not for me, it's for a friend."

"That glasses kid?"

". . . No."

"Really? Cause you pretty much have like one friend."

"If somebody wanted to really get knocked out, like, there's no way they could stay awake. Not enough to kill anybody or get anywhere close—"

"Pussy!" Tits says.

Tits is standing over a laptop on a stool in our garage. When I came in the laptop was playing a tinkly GarageBand rhythm and my brother was howling into a microphone hooked up to the laptop in his best imitation of all the scream-o bands he likes and Tits and his other friends were looking at each other and nodding like "YES, THIS IS IT."

"Six Valiums. Or as we call it, Alan's mom's lunch."

"Fuck yaself!" Alan says from where he's slumped in the corner in his green hoodie that says THE WORLD'S BEST FUCKING SKATERS.

"Or, you know what? Oh . . . shit," my brother says. "Follow me. ONE MOMENT, CUNTS, ONE MO-MENT!" he screams to his buddies in his soccer hooligan voice. He drops the mike on the concrete garage floor.

"Hey!" Alan yells. I guess it's his microphone.

My brother goes into the house, and I follow him. On the stairs, he says: "One week they're like, egging your friend's house like a baby, next week they're scoring drugs from you. THEY GROW UP SO FAST!" He punches the wall.

"Ow," he says.

My brother's room is a refrigerator compared to my room. My room's over the garage and insanely warm even with the air full blast. My brother also keeps his room surprisingly clean, for someone with so many personality problems.

"This is NOT where I keep my stash. So if you ever go looking for my stash, don't look here, because this is NOT where it is." He goes to where he keeps his stash: third drawer down underneath a Phoenix Suns Western Conference Champions blanket we got for Christmas the year the Suns almost beat the Bulls. I was a very heartbroken six-year-old after they lost and more or less quit liking sports. Same thing happened when it turned out Spider-Man's Peter Parker was actually a clone and had to go into exile: I was hurt and abandoned comics. I get burned and swear off whole parts of my life. I miss comics more.

He reaches down past the blanket and pulls out a Ziploc bag containing two big pills. He says: "Roofies."

I don't respond, but I try to make my face say, "Jesus, I know you are a dissolute behavior problem, but come on, we used to take baths together, and now you're in possession of the date-rape drug."

"Fuck you! I don't use them. I'm not a fucking rapist."

I make a point not to change my expression.

"Some dude paid me for something else with a bunch of stuff, and this was some of the stuff! Anyways, you asked! You think I need roofies? YOU need roofies. Date rapist!" He throws the baggie at me. I don't catch it and it hits the floor.

"Think of it this way: by you buying them, nobody who will actually use them will buy them. I mean, nobody who will actually use them for date rape."

The disgusting thing is that from what little I know about them, they are actually perfect for what we're trying to do.

"How much do you want?" I say.

"Take them," my brother says. "Merry Christmas."

I bend down and pick the baggie up off the floor. As we're leaving his room, we hear Eric shout from down the hall: "Oh, for PETE'S sake."

My brother looks over and sees Eric sitting on the floor of my room cross-legged, playing Xbox.

"If you're gonna rape your friends, you should get female friends," my brother says. "You're a real sick fuck."

"It's called . . . roprophinol." I stopped by the computer in my dad's office to go online and look up the actual scientific name before pitching it to Eric. I'm probably still pronouncing it wrong.

"The date-rape drug."

"Well . . ."

"That's worse even than the baseball bat!" Eric goes to throw the controller in anger, then thinks better of it and sets it on the carpet in front of him.

"No it's not! If you think about it, it's actually pretty perfect. No human being stays awake through this."

"Right. It's the date-rape drug."

"It wasn't DEVELOPED for that, it just so happens that that's what some people . . . some really bad people . . . use it for. We could use it for good, here!"

"What good? I keep forgetting what exactly is supposed to be good about this. Either I fall asleep, and my life is abridged in this one little place, and it's true, yes, I can be unconscious, or I just suffer through it awake, or God knows what else, really, since my brain chemistry is undoubtedly . . . different."

I shut my bedroom door and come inside and sit down. "I guess all that's, like, fair. Completely. But all this is about is testing the limits of your . . . thing. Finding out what there is to find out about it without us being, like, scientists. I mean, we could go to scientists, but, like we've talked about . . ."

I think both of us get visions of The Man, in his black suit and dark glasses, transparent and unkillable.

"You say that it's not a power, that it's just this thing, but we don't know that. We don't know anything, really. Listen, if you're scared . . ."

"I am definitely not afraid."

"Okay. I don't like it either. I don't like it that it's, like, for date rapists. Freaks me out just holding them."

"Them?"

"Yeah, there's two."

Eric picks the controller back up, thwaps it against an open palm.

He says: "I have an idea to mitigate the creepiness: we both do one."

"Ha."

"I'm serious. I'll take one if you do."

"Dude."

"Come on. It's for science."

And that's how it ends up that the first drug I ever do in my life is a roofie with my best friend in my bedroom above the garage, late afternoon on a Friday with my brother still howling away downstairs.

We get cans of Dr. Pepper from the kitchen. We crack them open. Back in my room, Eric turns on the TV. A movie about frat boys trying to see boobs is playing on Comedy Central.

"So we just like, let them dissolve?" I say.

"I don't know. We should ask your brother."

I put mine in my Dr. Pepper can and Eric does the same. He swishes his around like you see rich guys swish drinks in cartoons. We watch a few minutes of the frat-boy movie. The frat boys are at the bank applying for a loan, which is somehow convolutedly an important step in getting to see boobs.

"Waiting for mine to dissolve," I say.

"Me, too," Eric says.

Now it's a commercial break and neither of us has taken a sip when, halfway through a commercial for the new Medal of Honor game, Eric downs his. Like, chugs the whole thing in one go as I have only seen my brother and his friends do in the backyard with beers before and after screaming "CASE RACE!" Eric belches righteously.

"You really can't taste it," Eric says. "That is deeply, deeply evil."

It now falls on me to down mine, so I do, before the movie is back on, though not half as fast as Eric did.

"Yech. I want to throw up. Not, like, because I'm nauseous, but because I know what's like. In my stomach right now."

"Affirmative. But throwing up would be . . ."

"Unscientific."

We watch the frat boys struggle to build a three-stage rocket, which I really don't get, and I don't feel any different. Then, suddenly, everything gets heavy. Not me, everything else. With a lot of effort I make it to my very heavy bed.

I wake up to Eric punching me in the arm. His punches do not hurt as much as my head. My head hurts a whole lot.

"Ow. Dude! What?"

Eric slumps back against the wall, his eyes splitting the difference between open and closed. It's sort of like when I saw him in his room, that day he told me to go away. Except that day he looked wired and now he looks, well, drugged.

"Lissenathat," he says.

"What?"

"Listen to that!"

I prop my head up. From the next room there are sounds of my brother and some girl doing whatever.

"While you've been . . . asleep," Eric drones out. He is, like, cartoon drunk. It's nighttime outside. I have this headache and I'm starving and still tired, but I do not feel anything like Eric looks and acts like he feels.

Eric raps on the wall with his knuckle, the wall through which you can hear my brother and some girl, at it. "When is it my turn?" he says. "When is it . . ." and he turns his head toward me, which takes an endless seven seconds, "my turn?"

"Did you sleep, dude?"

"Did not."

"You sure?"

"Yes! I have NEVER. SLEPT. I would KNOW. Every second kept following every other second. Sequentially."

"So . . . that's good?"

"I dunno! You're the one that wanted to do this . . . is it good? I tried to watch . . . TV. Couldn't follow anything. No, like, fun drug amusement. Just. A lack of understanding. And then . . . an hour or whenever ago. This!" Eric knocks on the wall again.

"Is it going away? At all?"

"No." Eric seems mystified. "What if I never come out of it?"

"You'll come out of it."

"You don't know that. You don't know that. We don't any of us know. You said that. And now I'm never gonna come out of it."

"Dude, you are."

Eric nods like a toddler, emphatic.

"You are. When my brother and his friends do drugs, Tits always freaks out, and my brother says they always take him to IHOP and feed him coffee and pancakes and he's fine. Do you want to go to IHOP?"

"Well, if it works for *Tits*."

"C'mon, let's go to IHOP."

"I mean, just do for me whatever you would do for Tits."

I get up, which makes my head really thunder, and reach out to help Eric up.

"Whatever you'd do in this situation for a really good friend. Someone like Tits."

I finally pull him up and his full weight falls on me. I am still half-narcotized and not super-strong to begin with, and we almost collapse into the Xbox.

"Sorry, forgot," Eric says. "My legs barely work."

Supporting a roofied Eric it takes twelve minutes to get to the bus stop. "We've got fifteen minutes until the bus comes," Eric says. "Take your time." We get there with three minutes to spare, so I get three minutes of Eric, his head resting on my shoulder, saying, "Tits is a class act. Real pillar of the community," et cetera.

The bus pulls up and I drag Eric on.

"Eulalio!"

"Eric, what's up, man?" Eulalio says. *"Estás borracho?"*

"Así así," Eric says.

At IHOP it's just us, a big table full of kids from our school, and a table with a Native American family. I recognize some of the kids from school as kids who put a lot of effort into everything. I'm worried they'll see Eric, sloshed-looking, dangling off me, and think, I don't know what. But they are way too self-involved to notice us. Their food is almost all consumed and now they're each getting up and making a little speech, it seems like. I don't get it but it seems too weirdly healthy and I have no doubt they will all get into their first-choice colleges.

We slouch into a booth and Eric tells me he's not hungry and I can order whatever I want, but when the waitress comes I order us both "The Delicious Dozen," which is a lot of food, and two cups of coffee, which are "bottomless."

"I'm not hungry," Eric says when the waitress leaves.

"You should eat," I say.

Eric says, "I thought about *TimeBlaze*. We should . . . shorten the titles. The titles are getting long. More colons than a proctologist."

I laugh at that.

"I'm the only one. Thought about that, too."

"What do you mean?"

"Of me. Of people with my thing."

"We don't know that."

"Sure we do. If there were others, they wouldn't have kept it quiet. They wouldn't keep it secret like I did."

I think of Brendan Tyler and his left-nut-worthy car and how if anybody else had what Eric had they would probably change their Namespot status to "Nicole Allgraden HAS SUPERPOWERZ YOU GUYS!!!"

"Or if there were, we didn't hear about it 'cause they all got . . ."

I think we both think of The Man again.

"Someday, when you have kids, you'll pass it on, and there will be more. It's a total genetic advantage. Someday, we'll all be like you."

"Wouldn't want that, necessarily," Eric says. "It's Crossfire."

I laugh and look away because Eric's made me sad. Over at the overachiever table, everyone is packing up. A girl tells another girl that she forgot her balloons. I see the girl, the one reminding the other girl, and she sees me. She has her hair tied back elaborately with ribbons and stuff. She's gone before I think to smile.

"She's pretty," Eric says.

"You mean that Navajo mom?" I say.

"Oh yeah, her. Just hook me up with whoever you think Tits would like."

When the food shows up, Eric makes it further into his Delicious Dozen than I do into mine. He drinks coffee before I would necessarily deem it a drinkable temperature. When the bill comes, I pay it, and think about how it's fine because it's all money I had allotted in my mind to paying my brother for whatever chemical solution to Eric's thing we were going to try. So I am paying for this meal with money I saved by getting free roofies. Eric is not the weirdest thing in my life, I think. I am.

Outside IHOP, on the sidewalk, Eric insists he's totally walking-capable.

"Are you sure?"

Eric nods, and it seems like a sober and collected nod. So I let him walk to the bus under his own power.

"It seems unfair that the hash browns are counted as one item in the Delicious Dozen," Eric says. "They're called 'browns.' Plural. As in, multiple items. So they should count each brown. Are browns the unit of hash browns?"

Then he falls hard to the pavement.

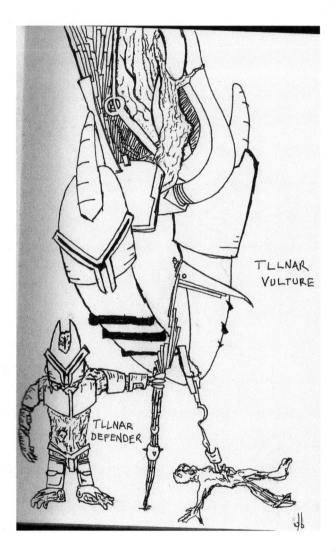

TLLNAR
VULTURE

TLLNAR
DEFENDER

"I thought about asking Tony DiAvalo to draw something on my cast."

It's a little dramatic to call it a cast. It's more like, I don't know, an arm brace. I've seen girls on the soccer team wear them. Eric's arm is just sprained. Some joints are sort of messed up but nothing's broken. He has some minor cuts and abrasions on his face where he hit the street. It actually looks like he gave a pretty good account of himself in a really cool fight.

"I know I said it already, but I am really sorry."

"I thought I could walk," Eric says. "It really felt like I could."

"You were pretty insistent."

"My mom hates you. I've been over at your house a ton and she gets called to the emergency room. So that's the great loss here, all the esteem my mom had for you previously."

"Did she?"

"I don't think so."

"Anyway. Sorry."

"It's okay. But can we put a moratorium on testing my limits?"

I say I guess we probably should.

This electric hum starts. Then the sound of a chain grinding against something. For the first time since Eric and I started sitting here at lunch, the loading dock door is sliding open. The light that's bright as hell out here at lunchtime even in late November spills into what's behind the door, which I guess is whatever's behind the auditorium.

The door finishes opening and the hum stops. Then this other sound starts, wheels on concrete and rumbling. All these big wooden slabs start rolling out on wheels, a bunch of girls pushing them. Some of the girls look like Cecelia and her friends, bigger girls with spiked belts and black T-shirts and hair they might've colored with highlighters. A girl who doesn't look like Cecelia and her friends, with black hair up in those kind of braids you might see at the Renaissance Fair, a girl who I'm 95 percent sure is the girl from IHOP, catches me looking at her chest. But mostly the girls look straight ahead, navigating these huge rolling pieces of wood that remind me of sailboats for some reason except instead of sails they have plywood sticking straight up, painted all over with a big-city skyline, some parts of which are more accurate, perspective-wise, than others.

"Goodbye, *Guys and Dolls*!" says a fat kid standing in the open loading dock door. He waves at the big wheeled cityscapes.

"Hey, Gary," says one of the girls, "why don't you, like, help, instead of like standing there?"

"Uhm, I DID help!" the kid, Gary I guess, says. "I'm just a little emotional right now, 'kay?" He has a high voice and a little bit of a Southern accent and a T-shirt that says IF YOU CAN'T RUN WITH THE BIG DOGS, GET OFF THE PORCH.

Drama kids. There are band kids and drama kids and the amorphous weird kids, free-floating nerds like Eric and me. There are other camps that could be called nerds but they're, like, the Anime Club and the Chess Club and they experience a lot of crossover with the drama kids and the band kids. You see the band kids practicing in the morning on the field where Eric and I staged our imaginary biologically modified troop invasion and I guess if you went to football games you would see them performing at halftime. But the drama kids you never see. You might have one or two in some of your classes and never know it until they stand up at the end of class and remind everybody that they have one of their plays this Thursday, Friday, and Saturday night. And they only have like two a year so you rarely get that reminder. The auditorium and adjoining classroom and whatever else is in that wing of the school is pretty much all theirs, their own little enclave where they could be doing any number of things, like sacrificing goats, but probably they just sing loudly to each other.

The big wheeled cityscapes pause right in front of Eric and me. The one girl and Gary keep bitching at each other. The girl whose chest I got caught looking at who I'm approaching 97 percent sure is the girl from IHOP comes over to us.

"Hey guys," she says, "we're gonna be painting out here for a while. It's spray paint so it could get kind of messy. Just, like, fair warning."

"Lunch is over in a minute," Eric says, "Aren't you guys going to have to paint kind of fast?"

"We get to skip sixth period," she says, "once every couple of weeks to help out with set-painting stuff. Our drama director made it so we can write it up as, like, volunteering."

Sixth period I have advanced chemistry, which is an exercise in torture because despite how much of Eric's and my stuff centers around biological modification and rips in time and the human genome perverted by radioactive ghosts, I'm terrible at actual nuts-and-bolts science. It's the only class I have that is neither easy nor something I'm good at. Eric has health, which he hates because it's easy. We're different people but we both have sixth periods that suck.

"Can we help?" Eric asks.

"Uhm . . . sure!" the girl says, looking pretty skeptically at Eric's arm brace, maybe wondering how much help he'll actually be.

"I'm Eric," Eric says, "and this is Darren."

"Hi, Eric. Hi, Darren. I'm Christine."

"Hi, Christine," Eric says. I'm not sure I want to be around these people or help paint and this is my only clean pair of jeans and if I get paint on them I'll have paint on my jeans for the rest of the week and it'll be a tell-tale sign that I wear the same jeans every day.

Christine looks at me. I don't know who I think I'm impressing and no one looks at my jeans anyway and fuck if I want to sit across from my lab partner today and have him look at me like I'm an idiot because I just don't understand valence electrons. I get up off the ground.

"Hi, Christine," I say.

"Guys, this is Eric and Darren," Christine says to her crew of girls in black hoodies and studded belts. We meet Marisa, Ashley, Claire, and another Ashley. They are nice and it doesn't seem fake. We meet Gary, who rolls his eyes at us.

Another guy, Ryan, comes out of the loading dock with some spray cans and some newspapers. He has big fuck-off boots and a newsboy cap and a white wifebeater. We spread the newspaper all around the rolling platforms. Pretty soon Ryan is placing his boots on the faces of bad local columnists in the pictures next to their bylines as we shake up the spray cans and cover the cityscapes in gray. The girls throw around gossip featuring the names of people we don't know.

"It's the cast party," one Ashley says, "it's for the CAST. What did she expect?"

"Kyle was being, like, the anti-Kyle on Saturday night," another Ashley says.

"Alisha has a lesbian switch she can like turn on and off," Marisa says.

"What is this for?" Eric asks about the platforms.

"A *play*," Gary says, like we're idiots for asking, like every tenth-grader knows that the first step in the process of making a play is to spray-paint some wood with wheels on it.

"Didn't you guys just do a play?" Eric asks. Some of the Day-Glo-orange flyers are still blowing around in the parking lot.

"Yes," says Marisa, and sighs so you can hear it.

All the girls get really quiet. The wind that's blowing the flyers around kicks up even more and with their hair blowing around they seem like war widows or something because they all start sighing.

"*Guys and Dolls*," one Ashley says. "The first ever fall musical in the school's history."

"There will never be another show that good. I guarantee it," Marisa says.

"Never," agrees another Ashley.

"It was miraculous," Claire says. "Everything came together."

Eric and I look at Ryan for some sort of masculine confirmation or denial.

Ryan shrugs. "It was pretty fuckin' good."

"I don't know how we're going to top it," Gary says, "especially with some . . . *experiment*."

"It's not an experiment," Christine says, "it's an experimental theater piece."

"Oh, right, THAT," Gary says.

Christine explains: "We do two shows every year. A play and a musical. Usually the musical's in spring and we spend the rest of our budget on it. This year our theater director Mr. Hendershaw did the musical in the fall so that way we'd have money left over and we could do a third play, after Christmas break. It's something he wrote himself. It's going to be amazing. He's a genius."

The other girls and Gary look away and keep painting. Ryan has gone to get his iPod out of his truck.

"It doesn't seem like anybody else agrees with you, necessarily," Eric says. I kind of want to hit him. I only ever deal with him when it's just us, for the most part, so I forget what an awkward dude he is around people.

"I don't know," Christine says.

"It's just . . ." Marisa says, "three PLAYS? I mean, it's never been done before, much less, like, something that's never been seen before. I dunno, it seems . . . controversial."

"EXACTLY, controversial, exactly," Christine says. "I'm not saying *Guys and Dolls* wasn't great, it's just, you know, nobody walked out of there going 'Wow, that changed the way I view the world,' you know?"

"It was supposed to do that?" one of the Ashleys says.

"No. I don't know. But we're artists, right? Shouldn't we ALWAYS want to do that?"

"I just like dancing," the other Ashley says.

"Mr. Hendershaw's piece has dance aspects," Christine says.

"Christine has suck-up aspects," Gary says.

Christine glares at Gary. What Christine has told us are called "flats" are now drying, completely gray, and the lunch bell hasn't even rung yet. Ryan pulls his truck up to the loading dock, leaves the driver's side door open, and blasts us all with ska music, the kind that, because of how bouncy it is, I can't imagine anyone but Muppets listening to.

"Ugh," Christine says to me. "I hate this."

"Yeah, right?" I say. We are standing in the gravel watching paint dry.

"What kind of music do you like?" Christine says.

"I dunno. A lot of stuff. You probably haven't heard a lot of it."

"Try me," Christine says.

"Uhm . . . okay . . . Styles Replay, Overlee, Manboy, Church Cancels Cow . . ."

"I LOVE Church Cancels Cow. Aren't they amazing?"

"They are," I say. "They are amazing." This isn't even the shit that my brother likes that I've picked up on, or the music Eric and I have decided would be good for the movies. This is the stuff I really actually like, not the things I like publicly.

"And Manboy . . . Oh my God. I haven't heard . . . what was it?"

"Styles Replay? Overlee?"

"Overlee."

"They're great," I say. "I'll burn you their albums," I say before I know I'm saying it.

"That would be great. Some of the people who were seniors when I was a freshman in Theater Division that are in college now, we still keep in touch. And they've got pretty good taste, but it's not enough," Christine says. "I'm so tired of ska and pop-punk and musicals, musicals, musicals."

"Me too," I say, even though I couldn't name four musicals if you paid me. My dad listens to jazz and classic rock and my brother listens to Christian scream-o and crack rap and country to be ironic and Eric listens to everything, one thing at a time, and I don't think he's anywhere near the genre of musicals yet.

"This is a weird question," Christine says. "Were you at IHOP really late on Friday night?"

"Yeah," I say, "that was us."

"I thought so!" Christine said. "We went there Friday after the show. Well, some of us. The musical has tons of people in it so we didn't want to—that was a whole other dramatic situation. Just once I want to go for French toast without being accused of elitism, you know?"

"Sure. When we were there Eric accused me of elitism like four different times."

Christine laughs and the wind blows hard in our direction.

"Well, there are lots of really fascinating sides to the abortion issue," Eric is saying to Claire and an Ashley.

"No. No. I'm sorry. No, we can't even discuss this," Claire says. I have no idea how they got on the subject of abortion.

The lunch bell rings.

"Looks like we're done. With this part anyway. Thanks for the help," Christine says.

"Oh, uhm, you're welcome. Should we still stay for sixth period, or . . ."

"Okay, well, let's think of this from God's point of view," Eric says. "Just theoretically."

"NO. NO. NO," Claire says.

"That's not very rational, and that's exactly what I'm talking about," Eric says.

"Maybe you shouldn't," Christine says. "You guys, I mean. I mean . . . I don't know if our director would be able to get you approved, and . . ."

"Right," I say. "Eric, we should go."

"But we get to stay through sixth period!" Eric says. "Legally! Right?"

I shake my head.

"Oh."

Eric goes to start packing up his lunch, now hyperconscious of maybe being late to sixth period, even if it is just health. I go to grab my backpack.

"I'll see you around, I guess. For that CD and whatever."

"Hey!" Christine says. "We're having this party this weekend. If you want to give it to me there."

"Uhm. Okay." Are you inviting me to a party, I want to say. But I realize that would be a stupid thing to say to someone who was actually inviting you to a party.

"Are you on Namespot? I can just message you the details."

"Uhm. Yeah. Yeah, I'm on Namespot."

"Awesome! I'll do it as soon as I get home."

"Okay," I say, knowing I should walk away, heading for my backpack as quickly as I can because if I don't I might screw it up somehow.

"Bye!" Christine says.

"Bye," I say, and look back so I don't seem completely subnormal, and to make sure the thing that I think just invited me to a party is a girl and not a trick of the light or swamp gas or a bunch of Drama Club flyers whipped around by the wind into a girl-shaped cyclone. It is, in fact, a girl, and she's waving and cute.

Eric is waiting around the corner, I think because he got the hint that if he stayed any longer one of our new drama friends was going to slap him.

"What did that girl say to you?" Eric says.

Most of the gossip you hear in school anymore is not about things that happened at school or even in people's bedrooms but things that happened on Namespot where it's impossible to detect sarcasm and girls nearly rip each others' eyes out over being bumped out of their friends' "Top Tags," and Eric and I have sworn never to join the cult, we would honestly rather have our brains eaten by spiders, as per Eric's worst-way-to-die.

"Nothing," I say.

I need to get to a computer.

I duck into the library. My sixth-period lab partner is just going to have to wait five or ten minutes to look at me like I'm stupid.

I grab a computer in a study carrel over by the dusty "Young Adult Fiction" section. I type "namespot.com" into the browser: It loads, thank God. Sometimes sites that are for purposes of entertainment are blocked by the school's firewall, but the librarians probably aren't the quickest trend-seekers and Namespot is something like the eighth social-networking site kids our age have adopted and then abandoned in the time I've been in high school.

As soon as the page loads I feel like a complete sellout: The front page is covered in banner ads for truly awful skate-punk bands and, look, I can enter a contest to be an extra in a sequel to a movie about a hard-luck inner-city dance gang. I hit JOIN.

I enter my real name. One of the million things that make Namespot obnoxious is the tendency people have to make their profile names cute or weird or off, like instead of Deandra, a girl might be DEANDRACAN'TWAIT4THAWEEKEND! Or a dude, instead of Chris, might be BMX_IZ_4_FAGS. I won't do that and plus how is Christine supposed to find me if I do? I guess people do it to prevent "stalking," which is a big preoccupation everybody seems to have, but nobody's going to stalk me. People just wish they were stalked. Given the option, they'd stalk themselves.

At first I start coasting through profile blanks, entering not much if anything at all for likes, dislikes, influences. (Influences on what? My Namespot profile?) But then I realize I want her to think I didn't just whip this profile up so she could invite me to a drama party, it has to look lived in, used. But what the fuck do you say?

For bands, I put the three bands I talked to her about, but then I think, no, that looks odd. I only like three bands? So I intersperse them with some other things, a band or two I've heard my brother mention, and some things my dad likes, like The Band, and some things I remember Eric rattling off when he was talking about his industrial phase. Then I look back at what I have and I think, This is weird, does this look like I'm too eclectic? Does this look like I'm joking? Then I think maybe Christine's got Namespot on her phone, maybe she's in class looking for me right now, and the thought simultaneously excites me and freaks me the fuck out: I have to finish this. For books I put a couple sci-fi authors, old ones, old enough to sound either cool or obscure, and throw Salinger in there for good measure. Movies: *Fight Club, Eternal Sunshine of the Spotless Mind, Sin City.* Not my favorite movies, my brothers', but mine sound too nerdy (the sacred texts like *Star Wars,* the original trilogy, and *Lord of the Rings,* and beyond that to be honest with you my favorite movies are theoretical ones that haven't been made yet and I think only people like me and Eric would make. You see how I can't write that). I leave relationship status blank: not desperate, not anything, an enigma. Yeah.

One thing it's missing, I realize, is an in-joke. A private thing between me and all the friends I have who spend all evening checking each other's profiles when we really ought to be doing homework. So under "Least Favorite Things," I write "Richard's dog." Who's Richard? What has his dog ever done to me? I have no fucking clue. But it seems like some dumb thing somebody would write. All the blanks filled in and tolerably smart and believable, I hit SEND.

The ancient school computer creaks and groans and the little world in the browser bar spins and finally the next page loads. "Add a picture." Fuck shit balls.

If I don't put one up, then my whole effort to make this thing look lived-in will be for nothing. Everybody has a picture on their profile. Narcissism is what this whole game is about. But there aren't any pictures of me, really, besides yearbook photos, and won't that look strange, unless it's my first-grade yearbook photo, in which case it'll be ironic, and I'm not about to be that asshole. I could put a picture that isn't me, that's Chuck Norris or George Washington arm-wrestling a tiger or some idiotic thing, but that's another kind of asshole I'm not chomping at the bit to be.

Then I remember: tucked in the bottom of my bag, waiting for me to remember to take it out and leave it at home, really, is this sketchbook, not my *TimeBlaze* sketchbook, but a nicer one I've used for what I guess I would call "real drawing." For like landscapes and people and sketches of hands and things like that. Things I do occasionally to try to prove to myself I'm not just doodling, but things that at the end of the day I'm just not good enough at or which don't feature enough head wounds to hold my interest. Inside that notebook is I guess what you'd call a self-portrait. I dig the notebook out, flip through, and it's there, between an aborted attempt to draw the mountains behind my house and a female statue's right boob. It's not bad. It's not good, either. I guess it just looks like I didn't really try, which is kind of what I want, I mean, if I'm going to be an asshole with his Namespot profile picture a line drawing of him done by him, it better be one where it looks like I went "meh" and scratched it on a napkin while I was watching TV. And it looks enough like me, I guess. Anyway, time is ticking, I've spent maybe ten minutes on this as it is. So without thinking about it a whole lot more I put the notebook page in the flatbed scanner next to the computer. I crop me, half-trying, half-finished me, out from between the shitty mountains and the floating stone boob, save me as a JPEG, and post me in my profile. I hit FINISH. The computer creaks, the little world spins, my profile loads. I am now part of the problem.

I expect that the nightmare is pretty much over and I am now findable by any cute drama girl who might want to invite me to a party for some reason, and I don't want to look at my new profile the way you don't want to look at anything horrible you've done, but I accidentally do anyway as I'm going to log off and I see, stamped across the top of this fucking monster, "MEMBER SINCE TODAY." The game is up. I could make ten thousand friend requests to make it look like I've been a Namespot jockey since way back, but it wouldn't matter. Member since TODAY.

I go back to class feeling retarded for doing so much work. But then I think, that's probably the same amount of work, the same amount of worrying about what nonexistent people and imaginary girls are going to think about what three movies in your "Favorite Movies" section say about you when put next to one another, and every other thing, I just did it compressed into ten minutes between lunch and sixth period.

The reason I know so much about Namespot even though I think it's repulsive is, Eric and I can't get enough of it. Nights at his place when I've forgotten to bring my Xbox and we're bored of populating the zombie senate of the postsingularity necroplanet, we go online and scoff at people's Namespot profiles and how unique everybody thinks they are. Sometimes we look at pictures of parties we didn't get to go to. It would be pathetic if we actually wanted to go to those parties, but we don't, so it isn't. It's sort of a making-fun-of-people buffet. It's almost too easy. People putting themselves out there convinced we'll be charmed by their overwhelming uniqueness. Well, we aren't charmed, Eric and I.

I get to sixth period all sweaty from rushing. I apologize for being late. The teacher tells me it may count as an absence.

My lab partner Ramesh gapes at me. I wonder what his three favorite movies are.

At my house after school I'm drawing the undercarriage of a mechanized bodysuit Eric and I are convinced is going to revolutionize the way people think about mechs in sci-fi but I'm distracted and I keep telling Eric I have to go to the bathroom. It's a little like when I was in third grade but I got skipped ahead to fourth-grade math and I got so freaked out being around older kids I'd go to the bathroom like four times a class. Nobody ever called me out on it to my face except one time a kid who sat in front of me said to the kid sitting next to him, "That kid sure goes to the bathroom a lot." The fact that my existence had even been acknowledged one way or the other was as good as being beaten down by the entire fourth grade math class, which I for some reason assumed was always ten seconds away from happening.

This time I'm not actually going to the bathroom, I'm going into the other room and really quickly opening up the browser and really quickly going to Namespot and logging in and seeing if I have new messages. Twice I don't. One time I have a message, but it's from one of those porn-website robots represented by a fake girl with a fake profile.

The third time I get back from the bathroom, Eric says, "Are you feeling okay?" I've been drinking a ton of Mountain Dew to make it more plausible that I have to keep going to the bathroom, and pretty soon, I actually do have to go.

In my house, my dad's home office, where the computer is, is right across from my bedroom, where Eric and I are working. My dad never works here. It's from the weeklong period when he was considering quitting his job and day-trading from home, but then all those day traders started killing themselves, and he decided to keep doing what he's doing, which I think has something to do with computers. On my way back from legitimately going to the bathroom, I break down and stop in a fourth time. I really quickly open the browser and really quickly go to Namespot and log in. This time, an annoying banner ad starts playing this scream-o music. It is loud and dumb and definitely not the sound of me peeing or flushing or getting more Mountain Dew. Eric comes in to see what the deal is.

"Are you on Namespot?"

"What? Yeah. Uhm . . ."

"Is that you on Namespot?"

"Yeah. Uhm. It's. Uhm. There's like, things you can only see . . . if you have a profile. Things on . . . other people's profiles. I thought it would give us, uh. More shit to make fun of."

"Alright. Don't get raped. There are an incredible amount of rapists on there."

"I don't think it works like that, dude. Some guy is not going to jump out of the USB port and just start raping me."

"That gives me an idea for a character," Eric says, and goes back to my room.

I hit REFRESH. A little envelope icon appears below my half-assed · self-portrait. I have a message. The subject is "party." It's from "christine's cliché screen name." There is an accent on the *e* in *cliché* and everything. I think about how every Namespot profile represents a unique and wonderful individual, and how Eric and I have maybe been too quick to judge, and how everything in the world is aggressively fine.

Drama party. I haven't been to many parties in high school so I don't know what to expect but I don't expect this. I guess I expect like a high-school-movie party, with lots of kids who look like they're thirty passing around red cups and a big kitchen island stacked with liquor and an Asian kid in a puffy neon jacket wearing inexplicable goggles on his forehead who pretends to be black the entire time. But there aren't any of those things.

What there is is a DJ, or really, a kid with two laptops and some speakers on a table. There are Claire and those girls I met earlier and Ryan, the guy I met earlier, and they're all in the living room where some couches have been pushed aside, along with lots of other kids, some kids who I recognize from IHOP, and some who, if they go to our school, have been holed up in the drama department the entire time, and they're all dancing. Like, really dancing. Guys with girls and girls with girls and occasionally guys with guys. That doesn't freak me out so much as the sight of people my own age dancing. Not at a school dance, either, which I also have zero experience with. A girl I don't know lets me in and I stand there gaping for a few minutes as a song I don't really know but am sure I hate plays. And a roomful of mostly girls and a few guys dance just to dance. I guess they look like idiots.

There is this one kid I notice, way nerdier than me or Eric, and he is dancing his ass off. I mean, not that I look nerdy, I think more than anything I try not to look like anything, to be not there to be noticed, but this kid looks like how I feel like I come off: fat and with a gross teenage beard and an anime T-shirt. Not that I am fat or have a gross beard or an anime T-shirt either. But this kid is just breaking it the fuck down. I am simultaneously grossed out and embarrassed for him and in complete awe. This is nothing I can process. I make for the kitchen.

Like I said, there's no kitchen island full of booze. Doesn't seem to be any alcohol anywhere. There's some snacks laid out, some pizza and sodas. I don't see Christine anywhere, and the only other people I know are dancing in the living room to what is now a song about butts. And even if the people I sort of know noticed me they'd only know me as the kid from lunch on Thursday with the controversial friend and we wouldn't have anything to talk about. I eat pizza, trying not to get any on my brother's button-down shirt. I am the only person in the house not writhing and sweating to the song about butts, besides the DJ who's playing the song about butts. Suddenly I want this to be a normal Friday night and I want to be in Eric's bedroom or my bedroom, the two of us swearing and drawing zombies or just fucking around with no one to impress. I regret telling him I couldn't come over because my dad was taking us to Outback. I would forgive him for not letting us explore more of his secret just to thank him for not being a weird drama person whose friend I want to make out with.

The back door slides open. One of the shorter, fatter girls I met at lunch the other day comes in, followed by Christine. Before I left the house tonight I realized people probably think about what they wear to a party before they leave the house, so I decided not to wear my usual black T-shirt and went up to my brother's room and took one of his button-down shirts. I am a monkey with a Namespot profile and a button-down shirt, I thought on the bus on the way here.

Christine definitely looks like she thought about what to wear before she left the house.

"He's an asshole," Christine says to the girl. "Bottom line."

The girl nods. "Thanks," she says, and Christine and the girl hug. I grab for a napkin to make sure my face is clean. The girl heads for the living room. Even having just gotten done crying she is more ready to dance than I am.

"Hey!" Christine says. "You made it!"

"Hey," I say, "yeah."

"Thanks for coming," she says. "These parties are getting really same-y, I thought I'd spice things up."

"Same-y?"

"Yeah, like, the same thing every time. They can be pretty fun, I guess. They're not like stupid football parties, with, like, jocks and beer and misogyny."

I don't know how she thought I would spice things up. I don't know where she got that from. It seems like to spice things up you bring a hardcore band to a party full of museum donors, or a hooker to a Vatican function. Bringing a quiet nerd to a party full of loud theater dorks does not seem like spicing things up. But I don't complain. Or say anything. I should say something.

"How are you?"

"Great! Really great. Sorry if you had to wait around in here. Must've been awkward. I had to help Becca . . . she just broke up with Mike. The DJ. He played Nathan Detroit in *Guys and Dolls* and he got a pretty big head."

"Yeah, I could see how that could happen." I don't see how that could happen. I don't know who Nathan Detroit is. In the other room, the song about butts reaches its conclusion and cross-fades into a song that was popular when all of us were in middle school. The cross-fade is courtesy of Mike who got a big head when he played Nathan Detroit, which you will agree is inevitable if you know anything about who Nathan Detroit is.

"So, Darren! What's your story?"

"What do you mean?"

"Like, what's your deal? What do you DO?"

I go to school, I want to say. What do any of us do? But I don't think that's the answer she's looking for. And the actual answer, that I am developing what is now a TV series culminating in a movie trilogy interspersed with books and graphic novels with any remaining holes in the epic filled in by a massively multiplayer online game, and my partner in this is my best friend who can't sleep and never has to—that answer I'm not ready to give yet.

"I, uhm. I read? And draw." I don't want "I draw" to read as "I doodle" so I think maybe I should say "I'm an artist" but I don't want to say "I'm an artist." I do think of myself as an artist, and I also think of myself as a science-fiction visionary and I also think I'd make a great boyfriend but I don't want to say any of those things out loud to anybody. "I draw, and—"

"RIGHT!" she says. "I have a confession to make. I like, looked at your profile for a while after I sent you the message about the party. And that profile picture . . . did you draw that?"

"Uhm. Yeah."

"Oh my God. It's. Amazing."

"Really?"

"Yes! Are you kidding? It's so good and accurate and I don't know. . . . You're a brilliant artist. If the rest of your stuff is even half that good, I'm jealous, because that means you're a brilliant artist."

"Geez. Thanks."

"Don't thank me! And you like Leonard Cohen? I thought nobody liked Leonard Cohen except for me and my mom."

Leonard Cohen is one of the artists I put on there to seem eclectic. I know about him because of my brother and my brother doesn't even really like him, but his ex-girlfriend who was a couple years older than him and broke up with him when she went away to college burned him a Leonard Cohen CD before she graduated. The only time I ever heard Leonard Cohen or saw my brother listen to Leonard Cohen was after she'd left when we were driving to the movies and he put in the CD and started crying and then made a U-turn and drove out into the desert so he could shoot the CD with a paintball gun. I try to remember what it sounded like.

"Yeah, he's so . . . quiet. You really have to listen," I say. "And the lyrics."

"I know, right?" Christine says. "Oh my God, you must think I'm some kind of stalker or something."

"No I don't," I say.

"Well, good. And didn't it say you'd only had a profile for like a day?"

I am found out. The beat of the song from the other room is so loud it's almost like a physical thing, so I think about trying to hide behind it until I can escape. She will think about how weird it is that she saw me at IHOP and then again on Monday and how I didn't get a Namespot profile until I told her I had one and how the stalkers she's joking about are real, and she's looking at one.

"Did your profile get hacked or something? That happened to Claire one time."

"No," I say, relieved to be given the out. "I've never had one. But then I figured, I guess I should get one. You know . . . for the art." I have no idea what I mean by that. "To be honest with you, I think Namespot is sorta shallow."

"I totally agree with you! It's like, everyone thinks they're so unique, like, people have Namespot profiles instead of personalities anymore, and Namespot interactions instead of REAL interactions, you know what I mean? And people fight more in real life about what happens on Namespot than they do about what happens in real life. When Claire got her profile hacked . . . THAT was a snafu," Christine says. When Christine sent me the message about the party, I went and looked at her profile. I think she put more effort into it than Eric and I put into the entire *TimeBlaze* saga. But she did use the word *snafu*.

The song that was popular when we were all in middle school fades out and another song fades up. A few people filter into the kitchen and start filling glasses with ice and water from a Brita pitcher.

"Hey Christine. Hey person," says one of the girls.

"This is Darren," Christine says.

"Hey Darren," the girl says. "Chris, just FYI, Becca is like, a wreck."

"I know. We talked."

"Okay, because she was dancing for like a second and then she went and locked herself in the bathroom."

"Are you sure she didn't just go to the bathroom?"

"She told me she was going to LOCK herself in the bathroom."

"Oh GOD," Christine says. She puts down her drink and looks at me. "I'm so sorry. Drama kids equal drama. We're more obnoxious than we realize. Hang out?"

I nod. I don't know what else I'm going to do. I'm definitely not going to dance. The song is a techno remix of a song sung by an American Idol champion from like two years ago.

"Okay," Christine says. "Be right back."

Christine goes, leaving me, the artist with whom she shares an opinion about the vapidity of Namespot, alone. I'm not bothered. I spend a few minutes putting handfuls of pretzels together with handfuls of M&Ms and eating them. It's something Eric and I do. I go to pour myself some Dr. Pepper. I have an unpleasant flashback and pour Mountain Dew instead. I eat more pizza. Eventually, I get bored in the kitchen, and it's awkward being the only person staying in there while everybody else comes and goes for water or food or to whisper secrets in each others' ears before going back to the dance floor. So I go out to the living room.

Mike is bobbing up and down in front of one of his laptops. His head does not seem especially big but he's wearing a baseball hat so it's hard to tell. He does seem like kind of a cock, just from the way he's bobbing up and down. People start hooting and stop dancing to look at something. Two girls in the middle of the room are making out. People are taking pictures. One of the girls is not really attractive at all and the other one is not *not* attractive. I wonder which is the one with the lesbian switch she can turn on and off. Camera phones click. Eventually that stops and I take a seat on the couch, feeling awkward as hell but not awkward enough to dance. Some of the girls are amazing-looking.

Claire comes out of the crowd and sits down next to me. "Hey, what was your name?"

"Darren!" I have to shout.

"Oh. Your friend was a real asshole to me the other day."

"Yeah, he's kind of an awkward . . . he's kind of awkward!" I shout.

"Is he here?" she asks.

"No!"

"Good," Claire says, "and no matter what Christine tells you, do NOT audition for Hendershaw's 'theater piece.' It is going to suck."

"Okay," I say.

A girl appears next to Claire and whispers in her ear. Actually, she's yelling, but I can't hear what she's saying. Claire giggles. "Yes! Absolutely! Yes! Bye, Darryl!" She and the girl make their way around the dancers to Mike's DJ table and lean over and yell in his ears. Mike nods. Claire and the girl high-five. Mike fades out the American Idol song and a song fades in that doesn't sound like it belongs here, all horns, but not the obnoxious bouncy Muppet-ska kind. The entire room goes nuts and everybody clears the dance floor. Suddenly where I'm sitting is really valuable space as everybody stands around while a few people take places on chairs in the middle of the room. Girls walk through the center and flirt exaggeratedly with guys. They're doing choreography. The crowd freaks out at every little motion.

As the tempo picks up, girls go into this dance with a lot of kicks, swishing their arms around to indicate what I guess are skirts they don't actually have. The cameras are out again, so that later when people are uploading their pictures to Namespot, images of two girls making out will go right next to pictures of people who are almost college-age kicking and swishing imaginary skirts.

Gary the fat kid is sitting next to me, clapping and cheering and telling individual dancers to "GO, Tyra! GO, Ashley!," et cetera. I look over at him.

"What's this . . ."

"The HAVANA DANCE!" he screams before I can even get the words out. "From *Guys and Dolls,* only the greatest production in the history of Theater Division!" Everyone outside of Drama Club calls what these kids do Drama Club. Everyone inside of Drama Club calls it Theater Division.

The horns are really blaring and now the dance is a fake fight. Guys I can tell are gay swing on guys who could fool me. The guys who could fool me swing back. There's lots of kicking and ducking under kicking. Some guys are kicking people who aren't there or ducking kicks from people who aren't there: I guess the entire cast of the greatest production in the history of Theater Division could not make it out to Nicole's house.

When I came in and saw a roomful of kids dancing I thought a little bit for a second that it looked like fun. Now I want to beat myself up for being anywhere near something like this. Christine aside I really want to be back in my room playing old video games with Eric quoting Weird Al lyrics because it's honestly less nerdy than this. I look for the kid in the anime shirt so I can ask him for confirmation on that. I let Gary have the couch and go back into the kitchen and then I work up the nerve to go out on the porch and tell Christine I'm leaving.

I slide the back door open and step out onto the back porch.

Christine and Becca are sitting on a pool chair. Christine is rubbing Becca's back. I startle them.

"Hey!" Christine says.

"Hi. Uhm. I think I'm gonna take off."

"Oh no!" Christine says. "I'm sorry I haven't . . ."

"Oh God," Becca says, "I'm like taking up your time, I'm so
sorry, I'm such a time-suck, God . . ."

"No," Christine says, "you're not—" but before she can finish Becca gets up and runs inside, not crying exactly but not far
from it.

"I'm sorry," I say, since we're apologizing.

"Don't worry about it," Christine says.

"Do you want to go talk to her, or . . ."

"It's okay," she says. "I think Becca's going to cry tonight no
matter what happens. Just one of those nights. Anyway, I feel like a
complete asshole for just, like, abandoning you to the wolves."

"Don't worry about it."

"Claire probably told you all sorts of wonderful things about
me."

"She didn't," I say, assuming she means "wonderful" sarcas-
tically. "I mean, she told me I shouldn't audition for Mr. . . .
Hendershaw's? Piece."

"Oh. Do you want to?"

"I'm not sure I even know what it is. And also . . . not really."

"Well, it's going to be amazing. But you're already amazing at
your own thing. You probably don't feel the need to excel in multiple things."

"I guess I never thought about it."

"Anyway, sorry for leaving you. I'm a terrible host. Come sit
down! Unless you really do have to leave."

I don't have to do anything unless it's not watch kids my own
age play-fight to swing music. I have to not watch that. I go sit
down next to Christine on the pool chair, wondering if everybody
who sits there gets their back rubbed.

"I'm a terrible host," Christine says. "Well, I guess I'm not really the HOST. I'm a guest. But, I'm like, the host in charge of making sure you have a good time, since I dragged you out."

"You're the host of our mini-party," I say.

"Right. Exactly. I promise we won't play any trance music at the mini-party."

"Oh, man! But if you don't play trance music, nothing at the party will suck!"

Christine laughs. She throws her head back and there is so much of her neck, all white in the moonlight. The moonlight is also glinting off the pool, which is probably freezing.

"Do you guys always eat where I saw you the other day?"

"Yeah," I say.

It is the last question I have to answer because it turns out if I keep asking her questions I don't have to talk. She doesn't mind talking and I don't mind listening, and it feels like we're out there a long time and not that much time at all at the same time, and we occasionally break from one of her answers to identify a song playing inside by its bass line pumping through the stucco of the house, and then rag on that song. She unapologetically mentions books. It turns out she has two classes with Tony DiAvalo and thinks he's a thoroughgoing d-bag. Her words, "thoroughgoing d-bag," not mine, but I agree. I realize with no small amount of shock that this is a conversation with a non-Eric person that I in no way want to get out of, that I am just enjoying rather than trying to minimize its awkwardness and length. I am interested on a level I imagine Eric is interested on in the things he gets interested in and learns everything about, learning and remembering with zero effort because I actually give a damn.

Pretty soon she has laid her head in my lap. This comes as a surprise to me. I start to get that standing-in-front-of-your-locker-telling-you-I-like-you thing, complete with unmanly trembling I pray she can't detect. She says something about when it was cool to tie flannel shirts around your waist and I lean down and kiss her.

I don't think I ever actively imagined what my first kiss would be like. But here's why I'm at least as big a nerd as the bad-teenage-beard anime guy: I'm pretty sure that whenever I thought about it in passing, it looked like a video game cutscene. In my head it was never at a real time in a real place. What I'm trying to say is I think I always figured it would happen on the deck of a flaming airship after I vanquished a multilimbed squid-god. This is not that. But this is great. It's real, and my neck really hurts.

"Is your neck awkward like that?" Christine says.

It is, so we reposition. Pretty soon we're making out and we don't stop to guess the songs based on their bass lines and after a while Becca comes out with some other crisis and Christine has to go inside and I say goodnight and take the bus home before I can screw anything up, Christine's phone number saved in the cell phone my dad pays the bills on.

I get off the bus and walk back to my house, jackrabbits scattering across people's lawns. My brother is sitting in front of my house underneath the porch light in a lawn chair. He is wearing over-sized sunglasses and no shirt, drinking beer from a can with an open case at his feet.

"Hey," I say on my way into the house.

"Beach party," he says, "Alan and them left, though," as though I'd asked him "What'd you do tonight?" He says: "What'd you do tonight?"

"Nothing."

"You go over to that kid's house?" He means Eric.

"No. Party."

"You went to a party? Oi, ja hear that?" he says in his obnoxious Cockney thing, addressing no one in particular. "Ee went to a fook-in' partee!"

"Yup."

"You want a beer?"

"Uhm . . . sure." I made out with a girl. I am drinking a beer with my brother on the front porch of my house. The old world I knew is dead.

He takes one out of the box and hands it to me. I open it and sit on the concrete. It's cold. I keep forgetting to be happy about what happened earlier, but then I remember.

"Is Dad coming back tonight?"

"I dunno. He left money. You can order something if you're hungry."

"I ate at the thing."

"Whose thing was it? I didn't hear about anything."

"Some drama kid party."

"Oh, a fag party."

"Fuck you. I made out with a girl."

"Ferreals?"

"Yeah."

"Nice! JA FUCK HER?" my brother says, and launches forward in his seat. His beer foams over and it's awkward and I think he senses it's not a good idea to be so completely himself in all situations. "Seriously, though. Nice. I'm through here. Top me off."

We drink the rest of the beers. There are eight left. It's the third time I've ever been drunk; the first time was a couple years ago when my brother had a Pimps and Hos party when my dad was gone and the second time was at my mom's wedding.

"I don't see that kid here much anymore. That kid."

"Eric?"

"Whatever. Big fuckin' eyes. Nerd. Yeah."

"Yeah, mostly I go over to his house."

"Good. You guys fuck with . . . Alan again, like that time? He'll kill you. I don't care as much."

"Okay."

"That's a weird fuckin' kid. He wanted roofies? Fuck is his deal?"

"He's like, I dunno, an honors student and stuff."

"That does not even begin to explain the roofies."

"You had them."

"You WANTED 'em."

"It was for an experiment."

"Fucked kind of experiment."

"No girls involved."

"Story of your life."

"I kissed a girl tonight!"

"Good. Me and yer pa were startin' ta worry."

Crickets chirp. I kill my beer and open another one.

"What fuckin' experiment?"

"Okay, get this: Eric can't sleep."

"Insomnia? Like *Fight Club*?"

"No, like, he can't sleep AT ALL." I think about trying to explain it further. Then it occurs to me I probably shouldn't have said anything.

"The fuck?"

"Or . . . that's what he tells me. I don't know. It's weird."

"You're fucking-A right it's weird."

"He's like, joking I think."

"You're fucking-A right it's weird." My brother is quiet for a long time, then he says, "Huh."

"What?"

"That's a weird kid."

"Yeah, he says . . . he says a lot of, y'know, stuff. He's got a big imagination."

"Huh."

I get up to go inside. Though I shouldn't have said anything, obviously, the armor on Eric's secret is that it's too strange to be believed. "Is that my shirt?" my brother says.

"Yeah."

"Well gimme it, it's freezing out here."

MECH
RONIN V 1.0

Christine is very quick to tell me we're not boyfriend and girl-friend.

"I don't like to get caught up in labels," she says.

I am very quick to tell Eric that Christine and I are not boyfriend and girlfriend.

"Where would she get the impression that you were?" Eric says. "We just met her at lunch the other day."

"Well, I went to this party on Friday night and she was there and we sort of made out."

"What? Friday night? I thought you went to Outback on Friday night."

I feel bad enough about telling my brother about Eric's thing that I tell him about Friday night but not bad enough to tell him I ditched him on purpose and definitely not bad enough to tell him I told my brother about his thing.

"I did but then she called me and I went over. It was this stupid drama party but she was there and that was pretty cool."

"What time did it end?"

"I dunno, I got home around one. . . ." I start to say "You would've been asleep" because for anyone else that would work as an excuse not to have called them, but I can't.

"Oh," says Eric.

What? I'm allowed to have friends outside of him, right? Especially when those friends want to invite me to parties and make out with me.

Christine is very quick to tell me we're NOT just friends.

"I mean, I definitely like you. I just want to take our time."

I am very quick to tell Eric that Christine just wants us to take our time.

"Hm," he says. "Does that mean she's allowed to date other people in addition to you?"

I don't know the answer when Eric asks. Christine just calls me up and gives me a declaration of who we are to each other the day after we go out for the first time, which is the Sunday after the party. We go to the movies on a school night. She drives because I don't have a license or a car. She drops me off at home and we make out in her car for a while before I go inside.

Here's the thing about making out: it's awesome. The other thing about making out is there's no talking and you don't have to think of anything cute or clever to say, and that's great. But there is absolutely no good way to get into it. Or at least no logical way. It just sort of starts. The first time we made out, at the party, I'm pretty sure we were talking about flannel. That is not sexy. Nothing about that says "make out with me." And when we make out at the movies it's all the sudden during a trailer for a new computer-animated kids' movie about talking animals, one of the twenty it seems like are coming out this year, this one about gophers. One of the gophers has Chris Tucker's voice and another gopher has Dane

Cook's voice and the movie is called "GoPher It!" Chris Tucker's gopher has just gotten in a gopher hole with his legs sticking straight up in the air, and he goes, "Let me out, I'm stuck!" which isn't even really a joke, and we just start. Later, when we make out in the car, Christine has just noted that at a certain spot on my driveway, the radio station we have on crackles and breaks and becomes a mariachi station for half a second. You are saying something inane and then you are not saying anything, everything you need to put voice to dumb thoughts you have pressed up against somebody else's set of everything they need to talk. Both of you are given permission to not have to think of what to say next. Maybe that's why we do it. Probably also we do it because like I said, it's awesome.

But now Eric has me worried that Christine is seeing movies on school nights with other dudes, so I text-message her and she meets me by the flagpole after school and I follow her to her car and we sit in her car and talk about nothing in particular for a while. So far I have only seen Christine at night. Afternoons are still Eric and me, and I'm planning to go to his house right after I hear it out of Christine's mouth that she's not planning on attending the opening of "GoPher It!" with Carter Buehl.

"So, uhm, I was thinking, we talked about, you had mentioned, like, we're dating, so does that mean you're like . . . dating other dudes?"

Christine laughs. "What? No. You're adorable. No. The whole, like, boyfriend-girlfriend scene kind of makes me claustrophobic, but that doesn't mean I'm going to be like, slutting around with other guys."

"Oh, okay."

"Why, did you have your eye on somebody?"

"No."

"It's that girl, isn't it?" Christine gestures to some freshman band girl who's heading out to or across the parking lot just like everyone else after school.

"No! But you are slutting it up with that dude, right?" I point to the fat kid with the gross beard and the anime shirt, which may in

fact be the same anime shirt as the night of the party, who is standing in somebody's truck bed, hooting.

"Oh, every night. Are you kidding me? He's deft in the bedroom."

"I'm glad we can be honest. Aren't you?"

Christine kisses me, and it's at a time that actually sort of makes
sense, a moment that seems to lead logically to making out.

I don't make it to Eric's house that afternoon.

"I feel bad."

"What? Why?"

Sweaty afternoon in my room with Christine. Theoretically
we're doing homework. There are math books and French workbooks open on the bed and mechanical pencils with little points of
lead clicked out of them but we keep ending up with our tongues
in each other's mouths.

I always forget which bases are which but I think so far I've
been to second base? Maybe just first. Whichever base is the base
where one night after seeing a black-and-white movie at an art-
house movie theater, and you did not know what to think of the
movie which was really long so you waited for the girl to weigh in
and she did and you agreed, after that you are making out in your
room with the girl in the dark and you tentatively unsexily straight-
up ask if you can lift her shirt up, and she sort of laughs but not
enough to ruin the mood, and when she actually does lift her shirt
up there is NOTHING that can ruin the mood for you, gazing at
something you have put more imagination into picturing than you
have the whole of you and your best friend's eight-movie sci-fi
saga, still in a bra but adequate, I mean, amazing, but adequate for
now, you don't need fuck else, and you act like you're in awe, too,
maybe embarrassingly so, completely treating them respectfully
like a museum piece, 'til you start to get greedy and another
embarrassing stupid unsexy question starts to form in your throat,
and maybe she senses it in your throat or maybe she gets tired of

the fumbly awkward museum treatment and she lifts her bra up easy as doing anything else and the clouds part and trumpets blare and any action by any frat boy ever in a dumb comedy is justified, completely, and all of the sudden it's like riding a bike, you just remember, except I never learned to ride a bike so I'll have to make up for all that time and devote myself to this. That's what base I'm at, as of two nights ago.

"Eric."

"What's the matter with Eric?"

"I dunno. We used to . . . I'm kind of the only . . ." I try to think of a way to say it that isn't explicitly "We're a couple of losers with no friends other than each other," but I can't think of one. "I haven't seen him in a while."

"Oh! You miss your friend." She makes a face at me like you make at a dog when it does a trick. She seems to do this a lot when I have visible emotions.

"I mean . . ."

"Well, you guys should hang out more. I mean, I'm not trying to take you away from your friend."

"I know. Yeah. He doesn't have, like, a lot of other friends."

"I feel bad now. I didn't mean to be like, depriving him of you . . ."

"You're not! You're not. It's nothing you're doing. I just have to like, make a point of seeing him." I'm not used to doing that. Negotiating more than one person's attention. "Y'know. Dude stuff."

"Okay."

"But it's not anything you're doing. Like, at all. This is . . . this is amazing."

"Us, you mean?"

"No, your French homework. Yes of course us."

"Ohh." That puppy face again. We kiss. "Hang out with your friend," she says. "Everybody needs guy time." She laughs. I laugh. We kiss some more. She starts taking off my clothes, and I start taking off her clothes, but she's taking her clothes off faster than I can keep up with and I'm really more of a hindrance.

"Whoa, naked girl," I say. It's sort of a joke but it's also my sincere God's honest feeling. The naked girl laughs at my remark and then she's all over me. You can guess what happens next even if I can't, in the moment, it comes as a complete and total surprise. I get to another base without even trying. And another. How many bases are there? I hope my brother's not home. I hope my dad's not home. Actually, I kind of hope my brother's home. Is that weird? I should stop thinking about this right now, I think. I use the naked girl to distract myself. It's pretty easy.

The naked girl scoots off of me and I go to say something about how fucking floored I am by the whole of everything that's going on right now, but I think I might talk as much when I'm not supposed to as I don't when I am, so I stop myself, and the naked girl is reaching into her purse and pulling out what looks like, yes, is in fact a condom. I schlubbed into my bedroom today a boy, I think, and it is entirely possible I will leave it a man. If I ever leave. Don't want to if I don't have to, the way this is turning out.

In the headlights of this moment I stop to think about who keeps condoms in their purse, and some part of that must read on my face because the naked girl says, "I'm not a whore, I just figured we were coming up on this." We were? I guess we were. Of course we were. I was pushing and conniving and manipulating everything so this moment could happen, this is the sum total of my chess-game-like dating strategy, of course we were coming up on this, I brought us here. I have forced her hand with my cunning make-out-when-made-out-with-and-talk-on-the-phone-when-called technique. I am a master. The naked girl is rolling a condom on to me. The naked girl knows I have no fucking clue.

So much skin. We're miles of skin in my bed. Whole landscapes. Hairy pointy jagged ones and rolling smooth ones. Scattered around the plateau of the bed, math and French homework. I won't do it. I'll hand in my math homework tomorrow half-done and just look into Mrs. Rammlyttle's eyes and she will just fucking know. We're miles of skin lying around in my bed after we're done.

"I should exercise more," I say.

"You did amazing," the naked girl says.

Two piles of exhausted fucked-out kids kiss in my bedroom, all soft and jelly-fied, and when they re-form in a few minutes, when they become solid, they'll be adults. Maybe one of them was already.

"Uhm, so what I was saying earlier? Yeah, I don't need to see friends or anyone ever again."

The naked girl laughs and kisses me. I kiss back and she breaks away and puts a bra back on, and underwear, turning back into Christine in the process.

"Soon you'll have all the time in the world to see whoever," she says, "when rehearsal starts up for the theater piece."

"Yeah? When is that?"

"Afternoons. Nights when the show comes up. It's going to be really intense since it's such a short schedule. So enjoy me now."

I nod hard. Ice water becomes necessary, and maybe Red Ropes or whatever's in the pantry. I ask Christine who was the naked girl if she wants anything from the kitchen.

I put underwear on. I don't think anybody's home and if anybody comes home it's not totally completely unrealistic for me to be around in my underwear at five fifteen on a school day. It's much cooler outside my room and with sweat still drying on me it's almost cold. I feel all rubbery and high and good. I don't know if that's what you feel like after sex or just after exercise, which I don't get.

The fridge is full of leftovers. I want to eat all of it. It is all owed to me, virginity-less sixteen-year-old adult. I pour a big glass of water from the Brita and drink it down and pour another one. Carrot sticks seem like something you could eat in bed after you were just naked with somebody in it, so I grab those. I think about eating a whole slice of pizza right there in the kitchen, but if I take too long and come back with breath that smells like pizza . . . I've never lost my virginity before. I have no idea what the etiquette is.

On my way back upstairs with the water and carrot sticks,

there's a knock at the front door. I look through the peephole. A balding dude in a pink polo shirt is out there, wearing sunglasses. Fuck it. I go back upstairs.

Christine is almost fully clothed now.

"Awww," I say.

"What?" she says.

The doorbell rings.

"Who's that?" Christine says.

"Dunno," I say, "some guy. He was down there when I was." The doorbell rings again.

"Maybe you should get it?" Christine says. Shit. Now everybody's going to be wearing clothes.

I get dressed, go downstairs, and open the door. A thrill of this-square-looking-adult-has-no-idea-of-the-depravity-I-just-perpetrated-up-in-my-bedroom shoots through me. It gets even stronger when he tells me he's from church.

"Your brother comes to our services. He told me, he told me something really very interesting about a friend of yours."

"What's that?" I ask.

"That this boy . . ." the man says, "that this boy claims he doesn't have to sleep?" He goes up at the end of this sentence like he can't believe it, so I just decide to play it like I can't believe it either.

"What? Oh, that was just like, something he said. That I told my brother about."

"Well, right."

"I mean, like, it was a joke even to begin with, and it kind of got, I guess, blown out of proportion or misinterpreted or. I don't know." It is unbelievable to even hear anybody else refer to Eric's thing. It's only been real between us.

"Well, we're not JUST a church. We offer a wide range of counseling and people who really listen. So if your friend feels the need. You know. Whatever his problem is. Drugs. Here's my card."

"Uhm. Thanks?" I want his pink shirt off my porch. According to his card, his name is Craig Haddaridy and he works somewhere called Lunaspa-Albans. "Thanks."

"Alright, then. And maybe we'll see you around sometime?"

"Yeah, maybe."

I think about calling Eric, but that's as good as admitting I told somebody. And I want him to be mad at me for not hanging out with him, not mad at me for spilling his biggest all-time secret and it ending up in the hands of church weirdos. Craig Hadarridy seems to think Eric is into drugs, at the worst. But still.

Then I remember there's a girl in my room, who was naked and probably could be again.

Christine has to be home for dinner so I decide to go over to Eric's house and tell him the news. On the bus I think about how I'm going to say it. Shouting "I DID IT WITH A GIRL!" seems too obvious.

I ring the doorbell. Eric's mom answers.

"Oh. Hello. I thought you were already here."

"Hi! No. Is Eric here?"

"I think he's off somewhere," his mom says, "behind the house."

"I'll go around," I tell Eric's mom, who I'm pretty sure thinks I got her son addicted to drugs that make him fall down and fuck up his arm, and who, taking that into consideration, is surprisingly pleasant.

Eric's house is on the edge of his subdivision, The Mesa At San Vista Hills. "Behind the house" is miles of desert, butting up against the Indian reservation if you go far enough. I circle the block and go down the dusty cul-de-sac that opens up onto not much.

On the other side of Eric's house's fence is a set of footprints, like the kid hopped the fence. More footprints in the dirt head off into the scrub brush and cacti. I don't usually tramp around in the desert or go outside much at all unless it's to walk or ride the bus between indoor air-conditioned places, but this is the new me, the man me, who has sex and tracks his friends into the wilderness with the sun setting.

When I find Eric he doesn't look like Eric. His shirt is off and his back is to me, he's facing the world like an Indian brave on a vision quest in a movie, and I sort of expect to see war paint on his face when he turns around. There isn't any, but his eyes are big and bloodshot.

"When I'm like this I see things and I don't know if they're real or not. So if you're real I'm sorry, but you really have to go. Please go."

"Can I help? What can I do?"

"I'm telling you," Eric says, his voice about two levels less nerdy than normal, "you can go."

"Are you sure? I can . . . We can . . ."

"No." Eric shakes his head. "But thank you. And Darren. This is assuming you're Darren. Don't tell anybody. I know this makes it harder. But you can't tell anybody."

I nod. Eric turns around like he hears something, but there's not really anything to hear besides traffic on the interstate maybe five miles away. But the silence and how totally he believes something's there has the effect of making the silence kind of terrifying in itself, so manly sex-having me turns and bolts and the kid who no girl has ever laid a hand on stands in the desert and fights imaginary God-knows-what. It's getting cold fast.

I run back to the house full speed, second time today I'm drenched in sweat even though it's winter, running even though there's no real danger it seems like, to anyone but Eric and even that's all in his head, and it's not like I'm running back to call somebody or tell somebody, I told him I wouldn't tell, I keep my word to him except when I don't. I feel like a fucking asshole for telling my fucking asshole brother and thinking just because it's something too crazy to believe that he couldn't find somebody stupid enough to believe it, but I will make it up to him by not running into the house and telling his mom that he's waist-deep in dangerous hallucination and maybe we should call someone but instead running back through the dusty cul-de-sac and straight to the bus stop and straight home, see you tomorrow. And his mom will just assume we're back there causing trouble in the scrub brush, even after it gets dark, because I am a bad influence. I told, I told, I fucking told.

During monsoon season these big thunderheads come in off the desert, like fleets of spaceships with hostile intentions. A lot of how I relate to the sky has to do with spaceships. When I was really little and scared of thunder, my mom told me to imagine they were Star Destroyers reentering the atmosphere from hyperspace. A lot of things ended up not being very great about her as a mom, but one of the good things was, she paid enough attention to *Star Wars* to get the details right.

So it's about four times as weird for me when I'm walking to school the day after Eric in the desert and there's a huge red storm hanging over everything. It hasn't been monsoon season for three or four months. There's a dim brown layer of smog over us always, but this isn't that. The smog is shapeless and you only really see it from far away. This is shaped like six thunderheads giving painful birth to each other. It's like the kind of storm that blows in off the deserts of Mars, probably. Except this storm never actually storms. It hangs there all weird and un-commented-upon by just about everyone in school, never releasing whatever's inside of it (rain, snow, skulls). By the time Eric and I are at lunch, it's dissipated entirely and the sky is maybe too blue.

"Did you see that this morning?" I say.

"See what?" Eric says.

"The clouds," I say. "It was like something out of *TimeBlaze*."

"Oh, yeah," he says. "I guess it was. Weird."

But we don't talk much more about it, because if we speak frankly about weird stuff, we have to talk about yesterday, and if we talk about that we have to talk about why I feel so guilty, and I'm not at all ready to do that. Maybe it'll blow away like that Martian storm, without ever spilling its probably terrible contents.

STEAMPUNK
PRAETOREUS

A typical day last year, before Eric: I walk home right after school. August through October and March through May my T-shirt is a sweat rag by the time I get there. When I get up to my room I take my shirt off and look into the mirror for a while, not in a vain way, just to see what the fuck is going on with my torso, scrawny and fat at the same time, has to be the worst torso for miles. Then I might turn on MTV, again not because I like what's going on there but simply to gape in wonder at what the fuck is wrong with everybody, and occasionally there'll be some stupidly hot girl on, writhing around on the top of a car. I go downstairs and eat everything in the kitchen and get an enormous glass of soda with no ice because it's cold enough from the fridge. I whale on kids and grown men on Xbox Live for a while, all of their voices modified by the presets to sound like robots or monsters. Once the headset starts to make my ears sore I go back upstairs to my room and turn on my clock radio, NPR, and listen lying underneath the fan if it's something interesting, and if it's really boring news, particularly from the Middle East, I might zone out and fantasize in a half-assed way about one or two girls from school. For some reason my fantasies work best if they're half-plausible and for some reason two girls from my algebra class falling into after-school lesbianism is more realistic than them throwing me any, so while a reporter drones on about the Gaza Strip I might think about a couple members of the girls' volleyball team making each other in the back of a Camry. After that and cleaning up after that I'll probably fall asleep until *Marketplace* comes on at six and foggily watch two syndicated *Simpsons* episodes or just keep sleeping until I'm hungry. If it's Thursday, my dad or my brother might knock on my door because we're going to Outback. If it isn't, they probably won't, and we'll each fend for ourselves in the kitchen or in the case of my dad and my brother, out somewhere else.

After Eric and before Christine, a typical afternoon is going over to Eric's house to talk about ideas and swear, and after Christine a typical afternoon is going over to Christine's house to fool around, and my phone that used to be a silent brick I kept in my pocket to remind me how lonely I was is now ringing every ten seconds with calls from Christine if I'm with Eric, in which case I usually go wherever Christine is, and with calls from Eric if I'm with Christine, which I usually ignore.

One time Christine calls and asks if she can come over, but it doesn't sound like a fun sort of coming over. She had a theater meeting after school so I just went home. I thought about going over to Eric's but I knew she was going to get out of her meeting at some point and call me, and I feel less bad just avoiding him altogether than going over to his house for an hour then leaving when Christine calls, so I take a way out of school that I know to be different than the one he takes and I catch the bus.

I'm watching a show about bear attacks when Christine calls. "Can I come over," she says, like words that are preceded by the words "I'm sorry, but . . ." and after I hang up this dread comes over me like well, here it comes. Sex after school with a girl that can stand you seemed impossible, and it was. The package was mistakenly addressed to you and the real owner is coming to get it. I settle in for a lot more bear attacks. Christine knocks on the front door.

When I open it, she comes in and basically collapses into my arms. She's been crying and will be again.

"The show is canceled!" she says. Her hair smells good.

"Yeah?"

"The administration, those fucking idiots, they say Mr. Hendershaw can't put up any new work. It's too 'risky.' It's not even THAT controversial! If they would read the piece . . ."

"Yeah, they're idiots."

"They ARE idiots. No one understands what he's trying to do, not the administration, not the parents, not the other kids in TD, fucking assholes . . ."

"Yeah, they're assholes." I've never been around Christine crying before. Her tears are hot on the collar of my shirt. I've been around Christine being around "other kids in TD" when they're crying before, so I just try to do what she seems to do, which is just agree with what the person says and then try to get them to look on the bright side.

"Well look at it this way, at least we'll get to hang out more."

"What? Fuck you!" Christine pulls away from me and whacks me on the arm.

"What? You said we were gonna be seeing a lot less of each other when you were doing the show and now you aren't gonna do the show so we won't be seeing a lot less of each other. That's all."

"It's not just oh, bummer, one less show. I've been looking forward to this since forever!"

"I know. Yeah."

"It's not fair," she says. "I've been wanting to do this kind of thing for two years now, this was my chance to do something besides, just like, the typical corny school play, and now . . ." She starts crying again. For a second I think of what my brother would say if he came home and found me embracing a sobbing girl in the front hallway. Probably something about how I rape lots of girls and she shouldn't take it personally. I don't want to be in the front hallway anymore where that sort of thing can happen.

"Do you want to go upstairs?"

"Fucking GOD, Darren! Can you not think about sex for like two seconds and just fucking listen to me?"

"I wasn't thinking about sex! I was thinking about your musical!"

"It's not a musical! It's a fucking experimental theater piece! You know what? I need to go. I need to talk to somebody who listens."

And pretty soon I get my wish and I'm not talking to a crying girl in the front hallway anymore, except instead of being in my room the crying girl is back in her car headed God knows where. I call her forty or fifty times and leave lots of apologetic voice messages and she's online later but doesn't respond to any of my instant messages. She didn't come over intending to leave me alone with my bear-attack shows but I guess I made sure she did anyway.

"Christine's okay."

I'm hoping to have lunch and not think about Christine. I've been thinking about Christine all day, hoping to catch her in the hallway and plead my case. I have the beginnings of an apology note in my English notebook. If things get really dire, I have the beginnings of an apology comic in one of my sketchbooks. I have fifty apology voicemails simmering in Christine's cell phone, or if not physically in her cell phone, then in whatever phone-company computer or server or satellite stores the world's voicemail. Wherever it is, there are fifty snippets of me saying variations on "Christine, I'm sorry, call me back." I wonder in negative repetitive patterns about whether or not she's listened to them or just gone through them one after another hitting "7." I've been hoping for what I can always count on, which is a lunch full of Eric and me debating the virtues of time machines versus wormholes, no matter how I've treated him. And now he's telling me Christine is okay.

"Huh?"

"Christine. I mean, she's nice."

"Oh. Yeah. Why do you say that?"

"She started talking to me via Instant Messenger. She said you'd had some sort of fight and she wanted to get an outside perspective on what you're thinking."

"What did you tell her?"

"That you're an asshole."

"Fuck you!"

"No. I didn't. I told her that you're really smart but you hide it, and as a side effect of that maybe you end up hiding your emotions as well, and so if you seemed less than demonstrative that's what that's about and you can't help it."

"Oh. Wow. How'd she take it?"

"Okay I guess. She said she'd think about it."

"Okay."

"She also said I was 'insightful.' "

"What does *demonstrative* mean?"

"You know what *demonstrative* means. This is what I'm talking about."

"Yeah, yeah."

"We ended up talking for the rest of the night. She stays up late. She's pretty nice."

"Yeah. I like her. I hope she doesn't still want to kill me."

Eric looks tired, I think. Then again, he did say he stayed up all night. Then again, he always stays up all night and has forever.

Christine sends me a text message in seventh period. She says we should go see a movie and bring Eric. I'm back in and not a terrible person anymore. Just like that, I get to have boobs and cyborgs and I don't have to choose.

We go to see this indie movie, *The Paucity of Feeling*. It's the sort of movie Christine likes, I guess because she's smart, and the sort of movie I say I like because I like to watch Christine being smart and I like it when she likes things, but I am coming to suspect that, despite my best efforts, I don't actually like these kinds of movies. It's playing at this art-house theater that used to be a real-people theater when I was a kid and my mom would take my brother and I there because it was the only movie theater in town when she was growing up, and I think because it was close to the mall and we could make a day of it. Now there are a bunch more movie theaters, big multiplex situations that remind you of learning your times tables (they all end in numbers divisible by 8: Desert Ridge 8, MesaPlex 16, Vista Crest 24), and three or four more malls, but this place is still the place you go if you want your girlfriend to think you're smart.

Christine picks me up first and then we pick up Eric. We are making fun of the hip-hop station's station-identification breaks before Eric gets in the car.

"YOUR HOME-HOME-HOME FOR TODAY'S HIP-HOP HITS," I say.

"He sounds like he's eighty years old. That guy does the announcements for every station."

"YOUR HOME-HOME-HOME FOR YESTERDAY'S RAG-TIME HITS," I say.

We fuck around like that waiting for Eric; it takes him a little while to stumble out of the house after I call him.

"Sorry I'm late," he says. "Dinner tonight was a total IQ."

Christine laughs and says, "I know what you mean. I was working on this French paper tonight . . . complete IQ all the way." Eric laughs.

"What does *IQ* mean?" I ask. "I mean, I know what it means . . . like, normally, but . . ."

"IQ. It's this thing we came up with the other night on IM," Christine says. "In honors history, Mr. Webber called Vietnam an 'intractable quagmire.' So we started calling things IQs if they are, in fact, intractable quagmires."

"Britney Spears's career. IQ," Eric says.

"My parents' marriage . . . IQ," Christine says.

"Ever getting our school on year-round schedule. IQ," Eric says.

"Driver's tests, total IQ," Christine says. "Not that you would know." She smiles at me.

I ignore the slight and try to play along. "Uhm, my brother, there's an IQ if I ever saw one."

"You're saying your brother is a conflict mired in complications which any form of struggle only aggravates?" Eric says.

"I don't think you understand how this game works," Christine says.

We pay for our tickets and go into the lobby. There's a café area around the concession stand. Marlee and Antonia, these two girls wearing big puffy hats that resemble muffins who don't go to our school but who Christine knows from their blogs, are sitting there eating pastries that look like their hats, notebooks open. Antonia flags down Christine. Normally I just stand around and look dumb while Christine and Antonia and Marlee talk fast. Tonight at least I'll have somebody to stand around and look dumb with.

"Ohmigod," says Antonia. "We just saw the Godard retrospective."

"Seminal," Marlee says. "SEMINAL."

"I've been meaning to see his stuff," Christine says, "but I haven't yet."

"You have to," says Antonia, "you absolutely have to."

"You really should, he's pretty great," Eric says.

"You know Godard?" says Marlee.

"A little," Eric says. "I went through a phase."

"What's your favorite?"

"Well, it's a toss-up between *Breathless* and . . ."

I lose the thread for a little while and focus on feeling betrayed by Eric, who is supposed to be a dude with me. Then I see my window.

". . . just like Kurosawa's *Hidden Fortress* was ripped off by Lucas with *Star Wars*," Eric says.

"Speaking of *Star Wars*, did you guys know that in the first draft of the script, Luke Skywalker was called Annakin Starkiller?"

Everybody, even my girlfriend, even my best friend, looks at me like blood just started gushing from my mouth. In fact, I think they would prefer blood was coming out of my mouth, instead of these stupid words that are trying so hard. In fact, I would prefer blood was coming out of my mouth, because then I'd have an out from this stupid evening.

"What film are you guys seeing?" Marlee asks.

"*The Paucity of Feeling*," Christine says.

"I saw it when I interned at the film festival," Antonia says. "You're going to love it."

They're called "movies," not "films," you fucking muffin-hats, I think as we make our way to Theater 2.

The movie, the "film," is a lot of shots of bridges and rosaries swinging from rearview mirrors and a guy with a beard is very mean to a French girl. It doesn't start where it starts or end where it ends for any particular reason and I keep wanting zombies to jump in from the margins of the frame and eat everybody but they don't. Everyone stares at the ocean for two hours, which forces us to as well, even if we don't want to, even if we would rather watch a thing in which a thing happens.

Usually when these movies are over I wait for Christine to

weigh in and if she hated it I hate it with her and if she liked it I say, "Ah, interesting." But tonight I'll have Eric on my side, and we will be able to argue with the authority of two dudes who have conceived of a seventy-hour multimedia sci-fi epic that this movie was a piece of shit.

"Bradgate was right, for once," Eric says when he comes out of the bathroom.

"Yes, for once," Christine agrees.

"Who's Bradgate?"

"The film critic for the *Republic*," Eric says.

"Usually he hates movies like this and loves, like, dinosaur island movies," Christine says.

"But every so often, he picks an art movie to champion, mostly because everybody else is. He gave this one a good review."

"Which actually had me worried," Christine says. "But he was right."

"So you guys liked it?"

Christine and Eric look at each other.

"You didn't?" Christine asks.

"Uhm . . ." I say, "it was interesting."

On the walk to Christine's car I listen as they dissect motifs and symbolism and mise-en-scène and Eric, whom I thought was loyal to clones and alien broods and movies that are actually, you know, about something, reminds me that while I jerk off and sleep, he stays up being interested in things. Christine drives and Eric sits in the front seat and the kid sits in the back.

A typical afternoon in the Eric/Christine/Darren trio goes like this: I'm either at Eric's house or Christine's house or one of them is at my house. At last it seems I don't have to choose, like my time is perfectly balanced. I'll be drawing the sails on an ultralight skiff designed to ride on the surface of the sun, and Eric will be contemplating ways we can cut down the length of our titles (we've gotten them down to just two colons) when Eric's cell phone beeps. Before Christine I never heard Eric's phone ring because I don't think it ever rang when I wasn't with Eric because I'm the only one who ever called. Eric flips his phone open and says to me, "What's a seven-letter synonym for *perspicacity*? Christine is beating me at this word game," and before I can answer, he's texting her back, not that I could answer. Or I'll be at Christine's house doing something to her I think I'm actually getting really good at, considering my previous lack of experience, and Christine's phone will ring, and she'll listen to the voicemail immediately after we finish, and she'll say to me, "Eric says you said the cutest thing at lunch," and before I can ask if Eric really described whatever thing I said as "cute" she's calling him back to find out what the cute thing was.

Or the three of us are together.

Or it's just me alone.

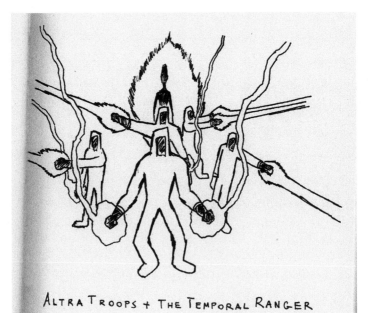

ALTRA TROOPS + THE TEMPORAL RANGER

9

She thought it was a seizure.

The way she tells it, Christine had offered to burn Eric a CD and did and brought it over to give it to him, and when she did he was locked up in his room and she talked her way in and he was freaking out, one of his "bad days," and he told her what he always tells me, which is "go and don't tell anyone," and she went down to her car and sat there for a while and thought about calling the police and thought about telling his parents, but didn't do either of those things. She didn't leave. She went back upstairs and went back into his room and waited him out. He was tripping. He thought she was a werewolf. He punched her in the gut. But she stuck it out and finally when he was coming out of it, sweaty and glassy-eyed and shaking, the both of them, her from being scared and him from whatever built-up tension the rest of us work out in our dreams, she held him, like La Pietà, that statue we learned about in humanities class, until he was completely recovered and realized what he'd done and apologized and thanked her for staying even though he had told her not to and thanked her for not telling anyone. Then they kissed.

Christine tells me first. I get one of those "can-I-come-over-we-need-to-talk" calls and this time I tell myself I'm going to be supportive and not say anything retarded or insensitive, whatever it is she has to tell me. She gets there and says we should go up to my room but not in a because-I'm-about-to-get-a-condom-out-of-my-purse way.

"He was having some sort of seizure," she says. And she waited him out, she says.

"Yeah, he gets those," I say. "He doesn't like to talk about it."

Then I expect her to get mad at me for never telling her this big thing about my friend that I knew, and I gear up to say he wouldn't want me to tell anyone, I was being a good friend, I'm always a good friend, but she doesn't get mad at me, which is when I know something is really wrong, and she tells me they kissed.

"Who kissed who?"

"I don't know, it doesn't matter."

" 'It doesn't matter'? That isn't something you say when it was just a mistake and it's never going to happen again."

"Well . . ."

"Well what?"

"Well I can't promise it won't."

"You can't promise you won't, because . . ."

"I kind of like him. Eric."

"I kind of like him too, he's my fucking best friend!"

Fuck not being able to sleep, now I have powers. I have eye-beams that fire pure rage. I have a black internal-combustion heart that never stops exploding. I have a red jealous streak that runs diagonally left-to-right across my chest and like Superman's crest it strikes fear into the hearts of certain people but in this case it's those who do not hold up their end of relationships. I am a meteor headed to Earth that was once a part of a planet made entirely of fuck-off.

I need to see Eric and have him tell me this whole thing was a hallucinatory mix-up, that he thought my girlfriend was an extraterrestrial queen he had to make out with in his fantasyland and he didn't know what he was really doing, just like when he slugged her. I'm out the door and halfway down the driveway, Christine running behind me.

"Aren't you going to lock your front door?" she asks.

"I don't," I say.

"Where are you going?"

"Eric's," I say.

"Do you want a ride?"

I wheel on her and if I really had those eye-beams I think I would use them. I end up letting out a half-sob, which is embarrassing, because fuck her, she doesn't get to see me cry. Besides, I'm not crying. For all she knows I'm going over to Eric's to bash his head in, even though I'm not, I'm going over to have him tell me what I need to hear so I don't have to bash his head in.

"I'm sorry," Christine says, but I'm halfway to the bus stop by then.

"I'm sorry," Eric says.

"Well, she thinks . . . she thinks you guys are going to be boyfriend and girlfriend or something." I laugh. Dudes. We can talk about this stuff. Eric doesn't speak, though.

"Uhm," he says.

"Fuck," I say.

"I . . ."

"FUCK!" I say.

"I really regret that it had to happen like this," he says.

"It HAD to happen? Nothing fucking had to happen!"

"I like her too! And she likes me! No one's ever liked me before!"

"No one had ever liked me before her either, hardly!"

"Right! So . . . so you know how it feels."

"I can't fucking believe this."

"You said it yourself, in a weird way, I've been alive twice as long as you, and in all that time no one's ever liked me, or wanted to have any sort of contact with me at all. When is it my turn?"

"So you would throw away our friendship and fuck me over for 'your turn.' "

"I'm not throwing away our friendship!"

"If you think we're still friends after this you're stupid. For all your books and interests and 'films' you're an idiot if you think we're anything except enemies after this."

Eric looks out his bedroom window. We're there, where it happened, the crash site.

"I'm really tired," Eric says.

"Boo hoo," I say.

I don't know every detail of what happened with Christine and Eric in Eric's room. But you can sure imagine a hell of a lot if you have an imagination that's used to getting inside of mechs and robots and thinking up political systems for other galaxies not yet discovered and how spiders would organize an army if they had to, and you turn it on something that's really small and you already know both of the people involved, know them really well, and know the things they could say and do that would hurt you the most and imagine them doing it in the most elaborate detail. You can flesh out the connection they have that you thought you had with both of them but I guess it turns out you didn't have with either of them. You know what their beds look like and you've seen them both with their shirts off. And as much as you don't want to be imagining it, that only makes you imagine it more, in sharper detail. You think, maybe when Eric and I were trying to imagine all this shit for our stupid fucking comic or whatever, maybe what we should've been doing is trying NOT to imagine anything. Because what this is teaching me is, when you try NOT to imagine something, that's when it really comes pouring out. If all along we would've just tried to stop ourselves from thinking of anything, we'd have been done in a night. A single sleepless furious night.

It instantly becomes epic-length. It doesn't stay just the one event. You've had it out of both of their mouths that they have every intention of doing it again sometime. So you get to imagine it live as it probably happens across town, again. It goes from a short film to a movie to a series of movies and comic books and an interactive online game.

And you can also imagine horrible shit that makes you feel a little better. You can imagine borrowing your dad's SUV and figuring out how to drive just enough to run them both down. You can imagine hiring your brother and his wacko friends to hunt them down and wild out *Clockwork Orange*–style and leave them in the desert. You can imagine all these things, but mostly you just die.

In the next couple of weeks I step back into a world with just me in it. Christmas break comes up. My dad likes to take us somewhere because my mom sometimes just shows up unannounced on Christmas if we're home. We drive to San Diego and stay in a hotel on the beach. My brother pushes me in the freezing ocean and calls me "fucking creepy" when I stay in a minute too long. For presents we all get each other Best Buy gift certificates.

On the drive back from San Diego with billboards for strip clubs and Sonic drive-thrus speeding by, we are listening to smooth Christmas jazz on a Southern California radio station, except my brother is listening to something hard and scream-y on headphones, and I'm not really listening, I am convincing myself that when I get home I will have an e-mailed apology/take-me-back notice from Christine waiting for me. I will splash my fingers across the keys, my user name, and splash my fingers again, password, and hit enter, and the little world will spin and there in my in-box surrounded by messages from casino porn robots will be an e-mail from "christines_cliche_email_address" that says she was really 100 percent wrong and wants to take it all back and my company, my boyfriend-ness, is better than all the experimental theater pieces in the world laid end to end. San Diego turns into desert, and we stop at a Sunoco to pee and gas up and so my brother can buy a thirty-two-ounce energy drink to give him the energy he needs to like, sit there and listen to really awful punk, then the California station fades out and my dad switches to classic rock as desert turns into our subdivision.

Right as we're about to get off the highway, in sight of familiar configurations of fast-food and hotel signs, something big and brown darts onto the road and into our headlights. My dad slams on the brakes but it's too late, we hit whatever it is, a dog or a deer. We come to a full stop and my dad pulls over to the shoulder.

"Fucking shit," my brother says.

Whatever it was is already gone from the roadway.

"Jesus," my dad says, and puts the car in gear.

When the SUV hits the end of our driveway the classic rock on the radio changes briefly, mysteriously, to mariachi then back into classic rock and the car is barely parked before I'm out of it and in the house running upstairs to check my e-mail.

There is no way I won't be getting an apology and take-me-back notice from Christine, by the way. All the mental work I have done composing exactly what it's going to say, all the heart I have put into wanting it, there is just no way it's not going to be there. It's like when I was nine or ten years old and this video-game magazine I had a subscription to was giving away a Street Fighter II arcade machine. I filled out the application blank and sent it out and as the contest came closer to being over I became more and more absolutely convinced I was going to win. I don't know when me really, really wanting to win became "I already won," and my mom did her best to manage my out-of-control hope. The fact that I did not end up winning the Street Fighter II arcade machine doesn't matter here. Willing one piece of electronic information to be in a place that doesn't even really exist is without a doubt way easier than willing an arcade game to show up in a crate on your front lawn through sheer force of want, and I'm older now. My powers of imagination and wanting are way more powerful, and add to that they're less focused on things like video games and more focused on grown-up mature things like winning back the girl who took my virginity.

But when the little world stops spinning there is not an apology notice from Christine. There are the anticipated messages from the casino porn robots and there are also fifteen messages from Eric. None of them have subject lines and they all have images attached. I open them one by one.

Attached to the blank e-mails are pictures of Eric and Christine, Christine and Eric among her friends she knows from blogs, the college kids she knew when they were seniors in Theater Division. Cutesy artsy pictures Christine's friends who make photo-zines have taken. Eric and Christine flash concert tickets. Christine dances with hipsters to live music in a tiny art gallery/music venue. Christine and Eric kiss in a booth at IHOP. Eric and a guy I don't know with a scruffy beard smoke cigarettes. All the guys who aren't Eric are like seven feet tall and have beards. He looks ridiculous, like a nerd pet they keep around to amuse them. Christine and the nerd pet kiss in a parking lot. At first I think maybe he's accidentally sent them to me but the time stamps show they were all sent hours apart from one another, nice and intentional.

It is so out of character that for a minute I imagine one of Christine's friends has a garage where they disassembled Eric and modified him into somebody who would do something like this. But in a world where my best friend and girlfriend start fucking, I believe there is nothing so bad that it won't happen to me, and I believe this instantly.

I guess it is only a little bit of a surprise that people have these hidden personality explosions where they turn out to be someone entirely different than who you thought they were. When I was like ten, my mom kind of went haywire. She realized that what she'd always really wanted to do was, not be an artist exactly, but live around artists and have the sort of lack of attachment or responsibility that an artist has. She wanted to start a whole new life with those kinds of rules, or lack thereof, and so instead of moving anywhere she just started living like that in the middle of having a husband and two kids. My parents got divorced, my dad got us, and my mom drove east. She met a guy in Atlanta and they got married in Palm Springs. As a general rule my dad is not huge on knowing where we are all the time, but when my brother and I went to my mom's wedding we had to call every half an hour and check in.

So it's not surprising to me that people can just blow up and change or I guess reveal who they always were, it's just disappointing that the people who stay the same are people like my brother or Cecelia Martin and the people who change or I guess peel back their façade are the people who you thought were the good ones.

I go downstairs and out into the garage to get a case of soda to put in the fridge. There's a mark on the front of my dad's SUV where he hit the animal on the road. There's no blood or gore, just a big yellow stain like we hit America's biggest bug. I don't like to think about what angle we would've had to hit something at for it to leave a mark like that. And also, we hit a mammal, a pretty big one, not an insect. I think. I wasn't paying much attention. I was in my head building a world where everything is back to normal that felt so real for a second I thought I could step into it.

In fourth period our first day back I have to run a class survey up to the office. I want it to take as long as possible. I'm in no hurry to get back to Mr. Webber's history class because I guess he got in trouble for showing us too many movies last semester so now he's pledged to lecture all day every day and he would clearly rather be running *Glory* or a Ken Burns documentary and you can feel him boring himself. So I walk around the side of the school and Christine and Eric are sitting in the loading bay. Christine is sharing Eric's enormous lunch, which he's not supposed to be here eating until next period, fifth period, when we both have lunch. I'm not going to stop or say hi, I'm just going to clutch my manila envelope and ignore them, but Christine says, "Hey, Darren," and stupidly, I turn my head. Just enough to acknowledge that they actually exist.

"You don't ditch class," I say to Eric.

"I am right now," Eric says.

"He's being very rebellious," Christine says. She smiles. She thinks this is all a joke.

I walk away, and Eric actually says, "That's right, walk away."

"Eric!" Christine says.

I actually, actively want to punch him in the face. I think about turning and running back and putting a sneaker in his stomach, and it's confusion that keeps me from doing it.

Sex with Christine has turned him into an asshole, I think, and that actually kind of makes me smile. Or maybe it's just hanging out with all the assholes in all the pictures I keep getting. All the muffin-hats.

That day after school Eric is waiting for me by my locker. Maybe Christine made him come apologize for being a real cock at lunch. Maybe he's come to do that on his own.

"Hey," Eric says.

"Hey," I say.

He looks skinny. Skinny even for how skinny he is. Behind his glasses his eyes are retreating into his brain. There's a scraggly sort-of mustache on his upper lip. I think maybe this is Christine's older friends making him into one of their own. But he has the same clothes and the same backpack and the same glasses, there's just less of him for everything to hang off of.

"So . . ." he says. "How do you wanna do this?"

"Do what?"

"This," he says. "We have to have it out."

"You mean like fight?"

"Yeah," he says, sounding totally unsure of himself, then again, "Yeah," like he knows he sounded like a pussy the first time.

"You're serious."

"It needs to happen."

"Fucking stop it. Stop e-mailing me pictures of you and Christine. What the fuck is that about? I don't want to know you guys. Go fool around and take pictures of each other and die."

What's left of Eric squares up to me. "Come on, then," he squeaks.

"Fuck you, you fucking mutant." And for the second time today I walk away and for the second time Eric says "Walk away" like he's seen it in an action movie.

My life is strange and I don't know anyone in it, except my brother, who's still my brother, so it doesn't surprise me when he comes in the house that night singing an Irish drinking song with Alan and it doesn't surprise me when he comes up to my dad's office where I'm playing a space strategy game online and shoves a wad of paper in my face, he's just that kind of asshole, but what does surprise me is what's on the paper. It's the dossier of a member of the *TimeBlaze* zombie posse.

"Tha fuck iz this?" he says in his British fuckhead accent. "Someone exploded yer faggit library all over tha droiveway, ya bastahd."

I push him to one side and run downstairs and out the front door and when I get there, sure enough, six months of made-up universe is all over the driveway, flapping in a half-assed January wind. Steampunk Praetoreous is stuck in the rubber plants. His cyberpunk counterpart is underneath the wheel of the blue recycling bin. Paper is everywhere and I'm completely fucking done.

I'm going to go back upstairs and tell my brother I will pay him and Jake whatever Christmas money I got in various cards from various relatives to have them go to Eric's house and push his eyes all the way back in his brain. Then I think of a better idea. Inside my junk drawer, next to porn I've printed off the Internet, I find the business card of that guy from my brother's church. I take out the phone I haven't had reason to use in a few weeks, and I dial the number on the business card.

On the third ring the guy picks up, and I remind him of who I am, and then I start talking about a boy who can't sleep.

"I didn't believe it either but I swear to God . . . err . . . I swear it's true."

"I believe you. I was ready to believe when I heard thirdhand from your brother. I was ready to believe even before then. These are interesting times. For things like your friend to occur doesn't come as a complete surprise."

"What are you going to do?"

"I can't be much more specific than I've been. Thank you for your honesty. If you need anything from me, anything, you let me know. And I hope I can feel free to do likewise."

"Uhm . . . okay."

"Thank you, Darren."

The creepy church guy hangs up.

I'd like to say that that night I dream of Eric being carried off by monks and nuns and ultrareligious freakazoids and burned at the stake at the top of a hill, but I don't. My dreams have no poetic justice, they're just mind farts. I dream about checking my e-mail. There's a thing where my brother and I are in a submersible in the ocean and he keeps trying to send text messages. I dream I'm fucking Christine. So no dreams about it but before and after I go to sleep I think about what I may have just opened Eric up to, and it never feels as good as I want it to. It feels pretty terrible, actually.

A typical day after me and Christine and Eric explode: I walk home right after school. I should start driving, but it's too late to switch into driver's ed and I've been bothering my dad to sign me up for the same driving school my brother took but he keeps forgetting. So for now I walk home and it's February so I'm not all sweaty when I get there. I go in the kitchen and eat everything. I feel a lot like human shit. I've started doing the occasional sit-up but it doesn't move anything around on what is still the worst torso in North America. I check my e-mail in my dad's office, but it's a lot like checking my phone: asking for disappointment, a good activity for somebody who likes the numeral zero, and blank screens, and no change. I go in my room and turn on NPR. I masturbate to scenarios totally unrelated to my life: weird fantasy specifics like cat women and Venusian slave girls. Afterward I fall asleep and wake up when it's dark. I have a couple hours of groggy useless energy after that and it feels like I could stay up all night. I've become really involved in this massively multiplayer game online. My character is a daemon lord whose right arm is a scythe. The rest of my squadron is ten-year-olds whose voices are modified to sound like bugs or robots. I always fall asleep eventually, and the days keep going like this.

In English we're supposed to be turning in our modern-day adaptations of *The Grapes of Wrath*. Creative assignments usually send most honors students into a seizure, because there aren't predefined rubrics for being creative, you're encouraged to do exactly what you're not supposed to do in any other assignment, which is MAKE IT UP, you're not even asked to provide a bibliography, and before long you have to put a belt in soon-to-be-valedictorian Alicia Henry's mouth to keep her from choking on her own tongue. But the *Grapes of Wrath* adaptation has a legendary, all-purpose solution: just make it about illegal immigrants. Some kid who was a junior when my brother was a freshman did it, and Mrs. Amory thought it was so great she used it as an example of the assignment for the next couple years, until people got the hint and just started copying it. I have one-upped everybody and made my adaptation, which is supposed to be a prose short story, seven to ten pages double-spaced, about Iraqi refugees. Plus, it's in screenplay format. Eric and I were briefly debating buying really expensive screenwriting software to write the *TimeBlaze* movie scripts, but we eventually decided against it and Eric wrote thirty or so pages of the first movie in a Microsoft Word document he formatted very specifically. I just take out the names DR. PRAETOREOUS and TEMPORAL RANGER and THE MAN and replace them with SADIQ and HADIR and TOM JOAD, whose name I decided not to alter for obvious reasons. And I change the dialogue and action, of course.

Mrs. Amory is coming around the room and I hand in my paper and then Chris White hands in his and then some girl whose name I can't remember but I think is in choir hands in hers and when Mrs. Amory gets to Eric, Eric doesn't have anything to hand in.

He sort of shrugs and tries to find someplace to point his sinking-in eyes besides Mrs. Amory's face. And Mrs. Amory stays there longer than she would if it were anyone else who didn't have an assignment to turn in, looking at Eric like he's right now undoing everything she knows to be true: first bell is at 7:45 and Pearl in *The Scarlet Letter* symbolizes evil and Eric Lederer will turn his work in on time if not early.

"Eric?" she says.

"Sorry," Eric says.

Though it was always a sticking point between me and Christine, that afternoon I'm glad I can't drive because everyone's cars are fucked. I walk through a parking lot full of rip-shit, mystified kids who can't figure out why their Jettas won't start. Ryan, the kid from Theater Division who is pretty much always wearing suspenders, is about to pull out of the parking lot in his old white truck. I look at him. He shrugs at me. I shrug back. A couple of kids in older cars are behind him, some of them packed with friends whose cars are bricked and need rides home.

The principal comes on the loudspeaker the next morning and

condemns what he calls the "car prank" and vows to ferret out the "parties responsible." I wonder if Christine's car still works. I think of how it smelled inside her car, like carpet shampoo and the weird nonsmell of the air conditioner. Then I punch my leg underneath my desk and try really hard to think of anything else.

Eric isn't in class that day, or the day after that. Then on Friday I am leading a squadron of bug-and-robot-voiced ten-year-olds into battle against another squadron of ten-year-olds that doesn't have such a sage older leader when my phone starts vibrating in my pocket. I tell BMXIZ4FAGS to watch my six and take my phone out of my pocket. Eric is calling me.

I should hold a grudge. It really seems like the right thing to do in this case.

"Can I come over?" Eric asks.

I should really be over people "coming over" at this point, knowing that when they call first they are coming to your house to break your heart in the first person. But there is really nothing the dude can say to me at this point that would surprise me in its awfulness. And also I'm hoping that like when I used to go over to his house with an Xbox and all the controllers shoved in a backpack, Eric will come over with a console that just has a reset button and we'll hit it and everything will be like it was in October.

We're in front of my house in pretty much the same spot where I told my brother about Eric that night.

"On Wednesday morning I got pulled out of class. I got called down to the principal's office, and there was this guy in there with the principal, then the principal excused himself and I was alone with this guy. And he said he knew about my thing. And he said he was from a university. He said he wanted to study my thing. And I asked him if I could have some time to think about it. He said I could, but that time was of the essence, that now that he knew about it there's no telling who else knows. I left and ditched the rest of the day. He came to my house that night and said he heard I ditched the rest of my classes, and I shouldn't do that, that if I started behaving erratically that would draw attention to me, and I didn't want that, did I? He said I should come with him right then, that there were people after me. I shut the door and locked it and when my mom got home I told her. I mean obviously not everything, but I told her this guy had been by and she said she thought it was a good idea, this college program. And it turns out that this guy had already talked to my dad and her, and they thought it was a good opportunity. He told them I was eligible for this early-freshman thing for high school students, effective immediately. And then I knew I was fucked because there's nothing your parents won't agree to if they think it's about you getting into college."

"Shit. Come inside I guess."

On the way into the house Eric stops. He reaches into a bush next to my front door and pulls out a piece of paper that's all wrinkled from being stuck in a bush and drenched by sprinklers then dried by the sun. It's some *TimeBlaze* art, still blowing around from when Eric covered my yard in it. A Thragnacian Containment Pylon. The Containment Pylons float in space at regular intervals around the wormhole that is the Thragnacian's charge. They opened the wormhole as a weapon in their war against the peaceful Albions, and the Galactic Conclave decreed as punishment that they should have to use their superior technology to harness the wormhole, and take care of it for the duration of their civilization. Eric folds it up and puts it in his pocket.

We go into the kitchen, maybe from force of habit. Eric starts closing all the blinds.

"I'm really sorry about everything."

"Yeah, what the fuck, dude? Seriously. I've been meaning to ask you what your deal is sometime when I didn't think you were going to say, like, 'We should have it out,' or something."

"I'm sorry about that. It was really stupid. I was saying and doing things I knew to be stupid. I'm really, really sorry. In light of everything that's happened you don't really have any reason to, you know, let me, but I was wondering if I could stay with you until this guy, this guy who I'm pretty sure isn't from a college, until he goes away."

"I don't know if that's a great idea."

"Oh."

"I mean, he probably knows where I live too."

"Why?"

Then I tell him. I tell him about the church guy and about the call and that I don't know how and I don't know when but the church guy probably resulted in this dude we have on our hands now, visiting Eric at home and handing his parents college brochures. And I tell him I called the church guy because Eric was being such a dick and that was my revenge.

"Oh," Eric says. "It almost worked."

"What almost worked?"

"Everything has been shitty. Everything. My thing. The bad days are substantially worse. I can still anticipate them, when they're going to be, my stomach starts to hurt and I get these headaches and that day I'll have to go out into the desert but now they happen more and more frequently and I feel shitty, I mean really physically shitty, pretty much all the time. So when I was doing all that stuff . . . the e-mails and whatever and just generally being a dick, I was hoping—Jesus, it sounds stupid—I was hoping you'd get fed up with me and knock me out. Like you said that one time."

"*I'd* knock you out? I'm the least athletic person we know, dude."

"I know, that's why I really had to be an unbelievable dick. I was thinking maybe you'd get your brother to do it."

This is such a dead-on echo of what I was contemplating a couple weeks ago, not in any real way, I don't think, but just in the holodeck of revenge we keep around to make ourselves feel better, that for a second I don't say anything. Then I think of something.

"You didn't have to start dating my girlfriend just to get me to get my brother to rough you up."

Then Eric is quiet. Then he says: "I didn't do it for that. I did it for all the reasons I said I did it. I wish I hadn't. But it helped me feel shittier, definitely. It helped me want to get knocked out, black out, take a few hours off, definitely. I felt really profoundly guilty and I still do."

I ask why he didn't come to Christine with all of this.

"I wanted to come to you with this, because this seems like it might be an adventure. And you bring adventures to the kids you make up comic books with. Christine, and those kids, those kids are more for blog entries and memoirs."

"Ah," I say, not really understanding what he means and also having to stop myself from automatically correcting him: *TimeBlaze* is, or was, not a comic. *TimeBlaze* is, or was, a ten-part movie maxi-series with the mythos filled in by comic books and graphic novels, culminating in a series-rebooting singularity at the end of the tenth movie, following which, using some technology not yet invented, all existing copies of all the previous movies will have their stories altered. I want to correct him out of habit, I guess.

"And also, I figured if I was going to come to you, which I knew I had to, I couldn't come if I was still, y'know, dating Christine, so I'm not anymore."

"You broke up with her?"

"I told her what the deal was."

The fact that Eric, poindexter Eric, could not only land Christine, who was dating someone (never mind it was me), but then when the time called for it up and drop her, her and all the nakedness she entailed, makes me hate him and admire him and be happy to be on his side all at once. Then I wonder semiselfishly how it all went down, how she reacted. And I think to ask and I realize I'm really not ready to talk to Eric about her. There's a clone of our dead friendship starting to grow in a tank full of pinkish fluid and I think talking too much about what happened, no matter the reasons for its happening, will flush the tank and leave the thing sputtering and dead.

So we've hit the reset button, but it doesn't clear the board. There are forces after us, stuff I called down upon our heads. But I have a best friend with superpowers, and days to fill, and rage to direct. And Eric has superpowers, and days and nights to fill, and a best friend with rage to direct. We have both seen enough and read enough to know that the guy who says there are people after Eric is probably the person in charge of the people after Eric.

Now we have our adventure.

Eric marvels at the plastic jar of hot wings in our fridge. It's big, like an economy-size pretzel-stick plastic jar. In fact, maybe that's what it was at one point. I think so, then we had a barbecue and my dad filled the leftover jar with leftover wings and now it's sitting in our fridge about half-empty. Me and my brother and my brother's friends have all made assaults on it, but we haven't come close to finishing it.

"Only a house full of guys has that," Eric says. And except for when my brother's girlfriend comes through or my dad's girlfriend comes through or until recently, my girlfriend came through, that's definitely what we are. (At least, I think my dad would call that woman his girlfriend. And I think that girl would probably say she's my brother's girlfriend, although my brother would probably identify her as "mah bitch" or "that cunt," depending on which accent he feels like shouting in.)

We're not sure where we're going to, but the right thing to do right then seems to be to put a bunch of snacks in a backpack and walk out into the dark. We're not sure where to, but before we go I throw on a hoodie. Eric doesn't have a coat so I let him borrow one of mine. My brother has left a quarter-pack of cigarettes on the patio table in the backyard, he's not even trying to hide his smoking from my dad anymore, so I snag it, and his lighter.

We ditch main roads and stick to side streets, which all have Native American names like Arapaho Peak and Native Crest, and come together to form subdivisions with names like Desert Pines and Mountain's Edge At Tapatillo West. I dig into sandwiches we brought, the meal I'd ordinarily be eating right about this time in front of the three thirty *Conan* rerun. I offer one to Eric.

"No thanks," he says, "I'm not hungry."

When I finish the sandwich, I throw the plastic bag away in a big dumpster on the edge of a construction site where a big new house is going up.

"Creepy," Eric says, "like, if I were a junkie who stumbled here from downtown, that's exactly where I'd sleep."

It is creepy, and being creeped out by it is actually kind of a nice change from being scared of this thing that's after us and we don't know what it is but we're very sure it's on our tail.

"Maybe he's a guy from the Vatican," Eric says, "and I'm supposed to be the Christ child or something, meant to bring about the apocalypse."

"Maybe he's from the government," I say, "dispatched to bring you to Area 51, where they'll run tests on you."

"Maybe," Eric says.

"But if we can imagine what it is, that probably statistically eliminates the possibility of that actually being what's going on. Like, if we can imagine it, it can't be real," I say.

"Maybe," Eric says.

I take out a cigarette.

"You smoke now?" Eric says.

"Not really," I say, "it just seemed like the right thing to do. You want one?"

"No thanks," Eric says. "At some point, I'm probably going to have to run." And his certainty gives me the creeps more thoroughly than the imaginary junkie in the gutted model home.

But eventually it wears off a little bit and we get to talking about what's happening on shows we both watch, whether the creators are staying true to what makes the shows so great or whether they've gone completely off the reservation, and we both got the *Maxim* issue with the girl who can phase through walls from our favorite show, *Superlatives,* even though we'd never, ever buy *Maxim* under normal circumstances, but some of the articles were surprisingly funny. And before long we're sort of around Eric's neighborhood and instead of turning back we drift towards his house, naturally enough and the whole thing not seeming particularly real. It's, like, five thirty in the morning and just a little bit of daylight is chasing the desert hares off people's lawns and as we're walking up Eric's front drive I hear the newspaper car coming around the corner. It's a sound familiar to any kid who stays up late in the suburbs: since there are no actual paperboys anymore, some depressing cigarette-y dude in a station wagon rolls around the neighborhood at this hour and along with the sound of his car you hear the thunks of papers hitting people's driveways, louder on Sunday mornings when the papers are stuffed with ads.

The paper guy still has his headlights on, and instead of orbiting the cul-de-sac for however long it takes to huck all the papers onto all the driveways and move on, the headlights freeze on us. The paper guy yells "STOP" and it isn't the paper guy, we can't see him with the glare from his headlights but it's safe to assume it's Mr. Who-the-Fuck-Ever, who works for the guy who works for the guy who works for the guy the church guy tipped off when I tipped him off about Eric, Mr. University. We aren't sticking around to find out who's on whose payroll. Eric was right, he has to run, and I shouldn't have smoked that cigarette.

We take off. We run through the side gate. Eric bypasses the big blue recycle bin but me, dumb and unathletic, I catch it right in the stomach. I hear a car door slam behind me, and shoes running on the driveway. Eric's up on the back fence, or back wall, big brown adobe bricks, with his foot slung over, reaching down to help me up. There's no time to resent the implication that I can't make it up and over myself but he's probably right, I probably can't, freshman year I would fake sick so I could not dress out in PE and read instead. When I'm up Eric hops down into the dry wash behind his house, a tributary of the one my brother and his friends chased us through. I remember being scared, but that was fun-scared. This is the real thing.

They say don't look back but up on the wall with a view of the whole situation I can't help but turn and see the dude tear-assing around the side of Eric's house, and another thing I can't help is thinking he looks a little bit like The Man, our unstoppable man in black, who may or may not be an actual human, who may be just a holographic entity. It's him, down to the sunglasses (at five thirty in the morning) and the way he almost runs right into the swimming pool but instead of keeling over or raring back in a funny slapstick way, he just stops short like there was no obstacle there to be concerned about, he just decided to stop. And when we go over the fence he doesn't appear to follow. We still run through the wash at full speed, but he doesn't follow, which is almost kind of worse. I picture him standing in Eric's backyard, waiting.

We come out a couple blocks away from Eric's house. We pant in the alley, me more so than Eric, who is in surprisingly good shape. I spit.

"What kind . . ." pant pant pant "of college admissions officer . . ." pant pant pant "fucking chases you through your backyard?"

"You don't get it," Eric says. "I'm REALLY smart."

We laugh, and have to start thinking about something to do today besides go to school or be at home. We are trying to figure out what time the mall opens when both our phones start vibrating. Nobody would text-message either of us at five-ish in the morning. We would, but both of us are in each other's presence. Christine? We take out our phones.

The text messages are credited to UNAVAILABLE. They say, COME QUIETLY.

We are under the bleachers at our rival high school. Going to our own school seemed like asking for trouble: it's a place we're known to frequent. Going to our rival high school seemed like the perfect way to throw him off the scent. Sitting on the bleachers seemed too visible so we're underneath them. No one is making out under here, nine thirty on a Saturday morning.

"My brother got in a fight with some Catholic-school kids here once, he said."

"Why here? This isn't the Catholic school and it isn't our school, either."

"Neutral location."

"Oh."

"Nobody probably ever said 'neutral location' and he just called it that later. He wants to be a samurai for the mafia or something. If the mafia ever starts hiring samurai I think that would be his dream job."

"Do you think if you had paid him, to like, assault me, he would've done it?" Eric says.

"I did think about it," I say. "I honestly thought about paying my brother. And his friends to . . . uhm."

Eric is quiet for a second.

"But not really," I say, not wanting to hear his reaction. "I didn't actually intend to do it or pull the money out of an ATM or anything. It was just one of those things you think about when you're really angry."

"That's it," Eric says.

"I'm sorry," I say.

"We need to find an ATM," Eric says.

"Show us the money," my brother says.

"Show! Us! The! Money!" his buddy Jake screams, cackling, and never looking away from my dad's office computer where he is watching a video of someone having sex with a pregnant lady.

Eric knew they'd ask to see the money up front, so we have it in the gym bag my grandma gave me two years ago with my initials stitched into it. I don't go to the gym, or participate in any athletics, so the only use my gym bag has gotten is the time Eric and I filled it with my dad's weights and threw it off our deck. We were settling a debate about gravity that had to do with whether or not Steampunk Praetoreous could realistically toss a half-ton proton charge off the deck of an airship before it exploded. (We wanted to be believable. It was the only way we could hope to change the way people think about proton charges and airships.) Other than that it has gathered dust in my closet, until now, the time Eric and I pay my brother and his psycho friends to beat on a guy my dad's age who may or may not be from the government but is definitely after us. Eric, and me for being with him.

"Who is this guy?" my brother asks.

"It's a long story," I say, "but basically, he's—"

"It doesn't matter," Eric says. "All that matters is he needs to get got."

Eric rips open the gym bag, revealing a very skeptical bank teller's drawer full of one-dollar bills. Enough one-dollar bills to make that bank teller look hard at the couple of haggard-looking teenage boys who are asking to be handed their entire savings accounts in one-dollar bills, but not enough to make her not give us the money.

Eric's idea is to make my brother and his friends feel like hired muscle in a movie. They *are* hired muscle, not movie-quality, but except for a couple of scoffs and a "Who does this kid think he is?" from my brother, the idea is working. Where else do people have duffel bags full of cash? Where else do they say "get got"? We are tickling a very specific spot on my brother's and his friends' teenage lizard brains right now.

"Alright," my brother says. "But we do this our way." Which is a stupid movie thing to say, but paying people to hurt other people is a stupid movie thing to do, so here we are.

We call The Man on the number he gave Eric. Eric tells him he wants to turn himself in. Gives him directions to a cul-de-sac that's a ways away from my house, up against the mountains, still mostly under construction.

We don't bring Eric. We decide that would be a little like bringing the kid to the kidnappers. And though it never gets said between us, one night not very long ago these guys did what they're about to do, except to Eric. If he wants a pass I can't blame him and he doesn't have to say it. But I'm going along, the project manager, to make sure they don't get distracted by drug scores or drunk girls or who knows, someone else to go wild on.

I have to tell them not to dress like the guys from *A Clockwork Orange*.

"But we get to do this our way!" my brother says as they're loading implements of fuck-you-up into the trunk of Alan's Altima. Two baseball bats: one wood, one aluminum. A samurai sword my brother got at the mall. A couple golf clubs. A coat hanger.

I tell them the masks will make them more conspicuous, and the suspenders will make it hard to run, if that becomes a thing that needs to happen. What I really want to say is don't, like, enjoy this so much.

"Let them," Eric says. "Whatever it takes."

So half an hour later I'm in the backseat of the Altima squished between Alan and Tits, who, because none of them have the actual masks from *A Clockwork Orange,* are wearing the faces of a Power

Ranger and Dora the Explorer, respectively. My brother is driving and Jake is riding shotgun.

"Five-oh!" Jake says as a cop car passes us in the other lane.

"Fuck 'em," my brother says, Eric's movie magic having worked on everybody, or maybe this is how they always talk.

"They can't touch us," Tits says. "We're untouchable."

"Touch my dick," Alan says, which is closer to how I imagine they talk normally. Jake and my brother had a twenty-minute argument about what music to play in the car on the way there, so we're about five minutes behind schedule. They decided on the *Lock Stock and Two Smoking Barrels* soundtrack. My brother makes up the lost five minutes by flooring it in a way Alan doesn't like, this being his mom's car.

We reach the cul-de-sac, which Eric picked based on his total knowledge of the neighborhood. Completely dark, no streetlights yet in the cul-de-sac itself, just some light leaking in from the street that leads to it, and the moonlight, and these red lights up on the mountains that are TV antennas. The red lights are so planes know the antennas are there and don't crash into them. They've been there as long as I can remember and when I was a kid and I asked my dad what they were and he told me, I imagined on the back of every red light a TV was glowing, showing what that antenna was broadcasting.

Everyone is trying hard to be businesslike, but can't help bailing from the car guffawing because somebody farted, and everyone agrees it's Jake except Jake. They get their game faces back on. My brother pops the trunk. Alan picks up the aluminum bat; Tits, the wooden one. Jake, two golf clubs, one in each hand. My brother, his sword. My brother puts on a *Phantom of the Opera* half-mask that disguises his identity, like, not at all, and Jake puts on a full Boba Fett helmet I'm actually pretty jealous of. They all adjust their suspenders. They cackle. I don't have a mask or suspenders or a weapon, just my phone, and I'm supposed to call Eric when it's over.

We have about four minutes until The Man is supposed to meet

Eric, and Eric alone, here. We have ditched the car up the road, out of sight, and we hoof it into the dark cul-de-sac. Everybody takes up positions in the dark half-built homes. I follow my brother, thinking about Eric's imaginary junkie as we duck through planks and blue plastic tarps.

"This is gonna be fun," my brother says. "I guarantee." We sneak behind a dumpster. My brother peeks out around it, I slide down so I'm sitting in the dirt, facing away from the cul-de-sac where The Man is supposed to pull up any minute. I am looking up at the mountains. My brother recites rap lyrics about snitches and what happens to them until there's the sound of a car pulling up and headlights chase rabbits out of the half-homes whose skeletons you can see just for a second. My brother whistles. A car door opens and shuts.

I should get visual, I think, in the movie terms we are all thinking in, I should have visual confirmation of what's about to go down. But maybe audio will do. Maybe I'll just sit here staring up at the red lights. That's what I'll do, I think, and I do, I stare up at the lights and I think, *You find out your best friend can't sleep and won't ever have to and you expect it to open up this world of heaven-on-Earth amazingness and instead it opens up a world where you have to sic the people you hate the most on a guy you don't know and get them to do what they would do to you given the right reasons or no reason at all, that is to say, kick your teeth in and laugh.* I will stay focused on the lights, I think, and not the sound of bone on new pavement.

There's more cackling and Jake yells, "Throw me the keys!" There's the sound of keys. A man's voice, low. My brother and his friends' voices, loud and wanting to swing, but nobody has yet. The Man's voice again. My brother and his friends, lower this time, more conversational, sounding less like they have a couple of golf clubs they're about to bring down on dude's head. The sound of a trunk opening. Alan, audible: "Hol-ee shit!" The Man's voice, my brother's voice, Jake's voice, my brother's voice. My brother and Jake's voices, closer, like they walked away from everyone else for a war council.

". . . their money back," Jake is saying, "and the money we'd make just selling the shit ourselves! And think of how much we could still keep."

"How do we know it's real?" my brother says.

"Alan knows this shit. You've seen Alan's mom. Fucked up. Alan knows pills, dude."

"How about we just fuck him up and take it?" my brother says.

"Look at this guy," Jake says. "I think he might be somebody."

A moment, then the sound of something sliding out of the trunk, the trunk shutting, the man's voice, the car keys, the car door, the car turning on and driving away.

Alan, again: "Hol-ee shit."

My brother comes around the side of the dumpster and says, "Change of plans, fag."

And that is how instead of assaulting this mystery guy and getting him to leave me and my friend alone, my brother and his psycho friends accepted, as payment for not fucking him up, a suitcase full of pharmaceutical tranquilizers, antipsychotics, and painkillers, hundreds of bottles with "Trial" written on the side, from the mystery guy. Who they said was really cool. Who they said didn't seem fazed by their masks or weapons, and knew just what to offer. Who, they say on the way back to Jake's house, cracking open bottles of pills, washing them down with whatever half-empty bottles of flat soda are rolling around the floor of the car, they should really invite to their parties because dude clearly has the hook-up. When we pull up to Jake's house my brother says he's sorry, but I gotta understand, right? Alan says he already can't feel his face, so they're in business, definitely in business.

I have to call Eric and tell him my fuck-up brother fucked up, and though we got a full refund, it's still the case that neither of us can really go home.

We can't go to Eric's house and we can't go to my house and we don't really have much in the way of other friends to stay with, at least I don't. But Eric does: Eric has those kids I saw him with in the pictures he sent me when he was trying to make me furious, Chrstine's college buddies.

"Those kids in the pictures you sent me," I say to Eric after we've dealt with the fact that my brother disappointed us, which isn't really a surprise but is still a bummer because we thought we could use the enemy we know against the enemy we don't, like in volume 3.4 of *TimeBlaze* where Dr. Praetoreous rallies the Hinterland Scourges to fight the malevolent Zethi Railroad Co. that threatens them both. I don't say Christine's friends because Christine's name is still this big hot word between us.

"Those kids," it will turn out, are Randy and Christopher and Benjamin and Chelsea 2 and Arthur and Larissa and Punk-as-Fuck Jess.

Eric has Randy's number.

"Hey. Randy?" Eric says when Randy picks up. "Hello, it's Eric," Eric says. "My associate and I are in something of a pickle and I was wondering if you could provide invaluable assistance," Eric says.

I look at him like, what is wrong with you?

"Really? Outstanding. We're at the gas station at Ray and Ranch Circle. Yes. We'll be here," Eric says. "And we'll buy you gas. And that won't even begin to make up the debt."

"Alright, then," Eric says, and hangs up.

I was looking through the gas-station magazines, but I give it up to glare at Eric.

"How I talk when I'm around them," he explains.

While we wait for Randy I page through a gaming magazine's E3 wrap-up and Eric buys Mountain Dew. I look at screenshots from a new World War II first-person shooter and think about me being dumb around everyone and smart around Eric and Eric being smart around me and smarter around Christine and even smarter around Christine's friends. I expect that when these guys roll up, they will look like college professors, they will flash library cards, they will wear glasses, they may very well not arrive by car at all but instead pull up on a tandem version of one of those old-fashioned big-wheeled bicycles. But when Randy finally does pull up (in a car), Christopher in the passenger seat, they seem dumber than all of us. Randy isn't wearing a shirt and Christopher isn't wearing shoes.

"Fellows, this is Darren," Eric says.

"Hey man," says Randy.

"Oh, right," Christopher says.

The "oh, right" seems like recognition, like one night after Eric was a part of their circle everyone was sitting around on the floor at somebody's place and Christine, from where she lay with her head in Eric's lap, got around to mentioning me like a crappy town where she met Eric and they escaped from it just in time. I think how good it is that Eric can be around these guys without Christine's having to be there, because I am not ready to be in a room with both of them and act like everything's cool.

I don't know how to think of these kids, and I guess if I could they'd want to kill themselves or change because they'd be labelable.

These kids, I come to find out, love their full names. Christopher. Benjamin. Franklin.

And they talk in this way I can't pin down, either, that sounds sarcastic but is actually sincere. Unless it is actually sarcastic.

I first notice this right after Randy and Christopher pick us up. We get on the freeway and get off by where the college is, and they take us to lunch at this place Cheba Hut, a weed-themed sandwich place which on the way there Christopher admits is "pretty lame but the sandwiches are really good," and if he means it the sarcastic way it sounds like he means it then he thinks the weed theme is really good and the sandwiches are pretty lame but it turns out the weed theme is pretty lame and the sandwiches are really, really good. And I start to figure out that as much as it sounds like the things they say are sarcastic because of the simplicity of what they're saying and their tone of voice, they actually really do unironically think that dancing is fun and local music is a good thing and so is making stuff, just things in general. And I wouldn't expect college guys who consider themselves intelligent to say so many things that don't have cynicism attached to them, but the sandwiches are only the first thing they're right about.

Basically something I think I believed without ever having thought about it is that part of being smart is not being able to start a sentence with a subject and then end that sentence by saying that subject is a good thing and actually mean it.

Eric's sandwich has sauerkraut which goes with the sort of little-old-man image he seems to have built for himself and he pays for all of our lunches to thank Christopher and Randy for "coming to our aid in such a gallant fashion." Christopher chuckles when Eric says this, toasting with his Styrofoam cup full of Mister Pibb, and Randy says "You're the best" while picking lettuce off his toasted sub which on the menu is called The Dank. Eric makes them promise not to tell anyone our whereabouts, and tells them we'll be "off your hands just as soon as we formulate a plan to spring ourselves from the situation in which we are currently embroiled," and they do. They probably don't think we're in any more serious trouble than maybe having been caught with some of the product that's depicted in murals all over the walls, spiraling organically out of Bob Marley's hair, raining down from a UFO, being dreamed about by Hendrix in a thought bubble shaped like a marijuana leaf. Tony DiAvalo should be apprenticing at the feet of whatever burnout da Vinci painted the wall in here.

Then Christopher says something about how quiet I am, then after we're done with lunch they take us back to their place, which they share with two other guys but it's still really clean, and it's theirs and it doesn't smell bad in the least, and there are five couches in the living room because "people crash here a lot."

Christopher is right, people do crash at their house a lot. Albert, one of the housemates, is in a band and they're off on tour, but he offers up the house to other bands that come through town and they do the same for him, I guess, when he's in their town. So Eric gets a couch and I get a couch and the other couches are split up at different times among members of Get Your Own Back, Tears In The Schoolyard, Andre The Client, and a singer-songwriter named Randall Coats. They're almost all really nice guys. If they're staying here it means Albert and his band are staying at their places in other states which means there are houses like this in a lot of towns all over the country, and I have to admit it's kind of cool. But for a while I don't want to.

A lot of time Eric forfeits his couch to these guys, since he doesn't need a place to sleep.

"Someone is trying to kill us," Eric says. "I mean, we don't know that for sure. In fact, that's probably the last thing he wants to do. At least to me."

"That must give you a lot of comfort," I say.

"Sorry," Eric says. "But for the purposes of self-preservation, to trigger our deepest self-preservational instincts, we have to think of it like somebody's trying to kill us."

"So what you're saying is, we shouldn't just sit on the couch reading comics all day?" Because that's what we've been doing since we got here: picking our way through the Preacher series, which Christopher says is his but we can totally read them if we want, in fact, we totally should.

"No. We want these guys to think everything's cool, and we're normal, and we want them to not mind having us around because having a place to go is the only thing that's keeping us . . . well, ALIVE, if we're going to think about it like we're going to get killed. Which I said was a good idea." He's doing that more often now, sort of rambling, and where before he would talk for a long time but everything he said would be a new thought and you understood it was relevant even if you didn't understand exactly what he meant, now he'll talk and not everything means something. And it takes him a second to get back into his Preacher book, a second of just sort of staring off into space.

I wish I could say that that's what's bothering me, that someone is trying to kill us, or capture us, or whatever. It isn't. It's more that this place kind of seems like the scene of the crime, the crime being Eric and Christine. Or if not the actual physical scene of the crime, the criminals' postcrime getaway flophouse where they brought their haul, spread all the money on the bed and fucked on it. Or any one of these couches for all I know. So Christopher forgive me if I'm a little quiet, it's me still being angry about it and feeling like shit for still feeling angry because I guess if I'm being honest with myself it's what I did when I was angry that brought us here.

All of the houses where Eric and I live are new, probably newer than either of us, but out here by the college everything's about as old as it gets for the desert, meaning one-story houses from the fifties and sixties. It's kind of cool, actually. Randy and Christopher's house is mostly shaded from the street by a lemon tree that must be older than anything in our suburb, the movie theater, the Olive Garden, our high school, any of it. Before dinner our first night, Eric says something pretty important that I somehow hadn't thought of up until this point:

"What are we going to tell our parents?"

"Well, my dad's easy. Your parents actually give a shit. That might be more difficult."

"Right."

"The Man said he was from the college, right? When he met with your parents."

"Yes."

"Great," I say. "He just gave us our out."

I tell Eric to see if he can borrow Randy's phone. Eric wants to know why I don't just ask to borrow Randy's phone. I tell Eric he's in better with these kids. Eric says okay.

"Randy my good man," says Eric, finding Randy in the kitchen, cooking: "Would you be so kind as to lend me your cellular telephone for a brief moment?"

Randy laughs. "Sure," he says. "Don't, like, call Asia."

We take Randy's phone and go out front since the house is kind of noisy because Randy and Christopher have a couple people over who are all in the living room playing Super Nintendo. My feet crunch on a carpet of leaves underneath the lemon tree. I dial Eric's house phone. Eric looks at me, biting one of his knuckles without thinking about it.

"Hello . . . Mrs. Lederer? Hello! This is Albert Praetoreous from State. I believe you spoke to my colleague the other day. . . . Yes! That's him. Yes. Well, as I'm sure Eric told you, some honors students from his school were visiting us today on an orientation field trip— What? He didn't? . . . Yes, I suppose he can be a space cadet sometimes, but he's also one bright little guy, if you don't mind me saying so. Yes, well interestingly enough, I confided to the students today that we had two foreign scholars who were meant to attend a longer orientation program we often do in the spring, which is this week, and they were unfortunately not admitted to the country. Visa troubles. . . . I know. I know. I completely agree, it has had a chilling effect on international travel. Well, I was saying this, and Eric piped up and suggested that he and a Mr. Darren Bennett take the place of these scholars in the program. . . . Right, I had that reaction myself initially, but I actually cleared it with our dean of admissions here, and I said to Eric, if it's alright with your parents . . . Yes! Of course. He's right here."

I hand Eric the phone. He gives me a panicked look. I wave at him like, "Just do it." He puts the phone to his ear.

"Mom? Yeah. Yeah . . . I'm actually way ahead on homework. Yeah . . . It seems really good. . . . Next Wednesday. Yes . . . I'm really far ahead on homework. No. No, yeah, it's okay. I'll come back and get stuff. Clothes and things. Tomorrow. Okay . . . Okay. Love you. Bye." He hangs up.

"Did they buy it?" I say.

"I think they bought it," he says. "That was a pretty good adult impression."

"Thanks," I say. I would've killed it in Mr. Hendershaw's "theater piece," I think to myself. Then I think how, not that I ever wanted to, but how if that whole Theater Division thing were something I wanted to do someday, now I pretty much can't, even though it's only sophomore year. And if I wanted to do it in college, I probably wouldn't, because I hadn't done it in high school and I would be way behind everyone else in terms of experience. And then it's weird to think that once I'm out of high school, that will have been high school. Like, the high school years, the ones everybody gets, those will have been mine, written in stone, unalterable forever. And I guess they haven't been bad so far. I didn't talk to anybody and then I made a best friend and then I fell in love and lost my virginity. Soon I'll learn how to drive. Soon I will escape from the clutches of evil with a mutant best friend and we will return to those awkward halls triumphant.

Eric looks alternately thrilled and scared at going out on a big rebellious limb like this. He also looks very tired. I take the phone back from him and pick out another number on the speed dial.

"Hey, Dad? . . . Hey, I'm going to that college retreat thing. . . . The college retreat thing. The thing I told you about. In Tempe. . . . Like a week, I think. . . . Yep, I have my phone on me. . . . Okay, uhm, love you, too."

I hang up. Eric now looks dumbfounded.

"That's it?"

"All parents respect 'college.' "

"I guess. How did you . . . ?

"What?"

"How did you come from that?"

"I don't know. How did you come from your parents?"

"Yeah, I guess you're right." We emerge from the darkness of the lemon tree and the whole lawn crackles underneath us as we go back into the house.

The weed-themed sandwiches turn out to be the only meat we see in the week or so we're staying with Christopher and Randy and their friends. Most everybody else and all the bands that come through the house are vegans. At first I think this is annoying, and I hear my brother in the back of my head saying "I hate fucking hippies." But everybody being vegan means everybody cooks, because I guess there's not enough good vegan food around, so everybody, the girls and the guys, all cook for each other. Five twenty-year-old people use their tiny kitchen seven or eight more times in a week than me and my dad and my brother use our enormous one. Maybe this week is an anomaly and they don't usually make this much food this often, but it doesn't seem like it. They seem to have their routine down pretty well. Eric doesn't complain or seem to notice one way or the other: he's eating less and less.

It gets pretty okay. The girls are cute and they all have projects they're working on. Sometimes the bands are here to play an actual gig at an actual venue but sometimes they're just playing at the house, which they don't seem to think is any less real than an actual gig, and none of the kids who come to the show do either. And they all talk like Randy and Christopher and some of them are actually being sarcastic but a lot of them aren't, and the girls are really nice, which I guess doesn't necessarily mean they like you, but it's nice when a cute girl in glasses who writes a sex column for the college paper is nice to you either way.

And kids do come to these house shows. And Randy and Christopher and James just let them in, and I'm sure if Albert were here he wouldn't mind either; in fact, he's probably in somebody's house in Tulsa or Washington State right now and kids are showing up to pay the band two dollars so they can buy gas. The most kids come for this guy Randall Coats' show, he just stands in the middle of the room, everybody sitting or standing around, and just him and his guitar, and his songs are a little sincere and a little saccharine for me but Eric leans over and says, "This would be good for the soundtrack," and I guess it would. I actually listen and it actually would.

All the kids know all the words to his songs and Randall Coats seems really happy, and you'd think it would be weird after the "show" is over, we're all still just here in the house, but it isn't, he just bows and takes his guitar off and hands it to a kid who wants to know about his tuning and he starts talking to kids.

Later I'm smoking weed in the backyard with some kids I've just met and granted sometimes this place seems like the scene of the crime but for a minute after passing the joint to the left everything loses its crime-scene aspect and these kids make absolute and total sense to me, and Eric and I, if we can help it, will return here one day and stay forever where Chelsea 2 makes journals she sells online and Larissa is getting her picture taken in a yellow raincoat underneath a streetlight and everybody can cook. Of course the show is in the living room and of course the bikes are in the garage and I will meet these girls and their friends and chase them through the bookstore. Eric and I will sit together in the back row of a class on poverty and if I miss a class to fool around in the top bunk of some girl's bed in a dorm Eric will have the notes and we will spend the afternoon picking apart burritos. We'll inherit this house and run a campus magazine out of it. Illustrated by Darren Bennett Written by Eric Lederer.

One day in the living room I get woken up by the drummer from Andre The Client talking on his cell phone to someone who I guess from his tone of voice is his girlfriend back home. The sliding glass patio door is a big square of light. I don't see Eric anywhere. I get up and bum around the house looking for him. While stepping over sleeping band members I think that it has been the same day for Eric since he was born, the same day since we met, the same day since he and Christine got together, the same day since I called the guy who works for The Man or who The Man works for on him, and it will be the same day when this whole thing comes to an end, reaches whatever conclusion it's going to. My phone vibrates in my pocket. I have a text from Eric reading DON'T WORRY. BAD DAY. GOING TO THE DESERT.

When he gets back I want to ask him if he can maybe see down the barrel of his one long day and tell me how this all works out. Not like I think he's psychic, but for him it's all one unbroken day, and while I couldn't tell you what's going to happen to me twenty years from now in a span of time all broken up by sleep, I could probably tell you, based on how my day is going, how my night's going to be. And since for him it's all one unbroken day I want to hear from him how he thinks it might end.

When I wake up from a nap that afternoon he's there in the living room and everybody from the band is gone. I remember there was something I wanted to ask him this morning but I don't remember what. On the coffee table, Eric has smoothed out the wrinkled picture of the Thragnacian Containment Pylon from my front yard. He's staring at the picture until he notices I'm awake. He smiles and says, I guess about the drawing, "We did a really good job."

I agree with him and before I can say anything else he's gone to take a shower to wash the desert off.

Aside from all the living-room shows, there are real shows too. The actual shows at actual venues are not much different than the living-room shows, it's the same kids and some of their friends, except now there's a raised platform and sometimes amplified sound. And when there's amplifiers there's usually more dancing. These kids really like dancing, in this sort-of-ironic-but-not way which is the same way they talk, the same way they do everything, sincere like sincerity is new, as surprised as I am to find out that they really mean it.

I don't dance. Eric I've never even seen in the same room as dancing, with the exception of the time we went to an arcade and tried Dance Dance Revolution and waited for each other to admit that we hated it and were exhausted so we could go play the zombie-killing games.

Even the real venues aren't what you would consider big concert spaces. Mostly we end up at this art gallery place downtown that also has shows in the back. It's called Circumference. And at Circumference on this particular night we're watching The Achievables, who are from Olympia, Washington, but before that the opening act is up. They're called Ten Who Dared, even though there are only eight of them. Eric has a good point when he says he could understand calling your band that if there were like, four or five of you, but eight is so close to ten all the irony is lost. This seems like a pretty good observation, and I'm repeating it to Chelsea 2, not necessarily giving Eric full credit, when she says, "Have you seen them?"

"No," I say, "not yet," because maybe that will make it seem like I've been meaning to see them, trying really hard to see them, it's just circumstances that have stood in my way.

"They're local," she says, which, I have come to learn, is a good thing.

"Oh," I say.

"Yeah, they're really good," she says. "You HAVE to dance."

I am skeptical and sure that when they are done tuning up their instruments the six guys and two girls onstage will not be able to do what numerous DJs haven't been able to make me do, which is dance. Well, okay, not numerous. That one DJ Mike at that one drama party that one time.

But when they start playing it's not weird or obtuse or arty or difficult to get, it's fun and simple and pretty catchy. And kids start dancing, and I guess it's not really good dancing in the technical sense but they commit really hard to it and it doesn't look intimidating. Chelsea 2 has her hair up in pigtails and as she moves around the ends of the pigtails bounce off her cheeks, and her cheeks have freckles, and when she grabs my hand and pulls me towards the center of the room where kids are bouncing up and down and side to side and girls are flipping their skirts around their ankles and laughing, I go with her and I feel like a retard and a spaz and all those other things but I sort of don't give a shit, and I think of that one time with that one DJ when I didn't dance, all those theater kids and Christine, and how different this is and how long ago that was except I guess it's not that different because when the song is over and the singer says "Thank you, we're Ten Who Dared and we're from Cave Creek" and everybody cheers, someone taps me on the shoulder and I turn around and it's Christine.

"I wanted to come say hi to you before it seemed, like brutally obvious that I wasn't coming to say hi to you," she says. "Besides, I miss you. Can we go talk somewhere?"

It's kind of cold outside but I'm all sweaty from dancing or whatever you want to call it so it actually feels nice.

"So how've you been?" I say, the words sort of catching in my throat.

"Okay I guess," she says. "I just really want to apologize for everything that happened with me and Eric. Everything just got fucked up so fast, and when he started acting really weird towards you . . . I mean, I couldn't understand it. I can't believe you're still friends with him."

"He has his reasons," I say.

"Yeah, well. It's good to see you guys. Even if you can't, like, talk to me. Where is he, anyway? I saw him when I came in, but . . ."

"I think he's smoking with Aaron and Paul by the fire exit."

"Aw, neat. Those guys love him. Everybody loves him."

"Yeah, it's cool. Your friends are really nice." I've run out of things to say, or anyway, say-able things, so I ask: "What about your theater friends?"

"Ugh, don't get me started. Some friends. Mr. Hendershaw came up for review this year for what the administration refers to as some of his 'questionable choices,' and they had this town hall meeting, and NOBODY stood by him. Nobody he didn't cast in absolutely every role they ever thought they deserved, which is nobody, of course, so everybody just, I don't know, copped out, and so it doesn't look like he'll be coming back next year. . . ."

She continues, and I don't particularly care about the theater kids, but now I'm really glad I asked, because something slides into place for me, and I really want to go back inside. Not to get away from Christine, she's fine, she can go or stay, it really doesn't matter, but inside are the bands, and inside is Chelsea 2. It's not like I like her, but I COULD like her, and I like what she represents. If I told her I liked her because she represents possibility, she'd probably hit me. But she does represent it, the same way Eric represents the fact that anything is possible.

ANYTHING IS POSSIBLE. It always sounded like a dumb cliché that escaped from a Disney movie, and it was the thing that I dismissed first when I started collecting what I figured were the opinions mature people have, that most everything is bullshit and you can't trust anybody and there is no magic to be had. But these kids are older than I am, they go to college, and they don't seem to think that everything is stupid, not everything. And Eric, whom I sold out over the girl standing next to me, proves that not only is everything not stupid but everything is possible, the world is movie-quality like we always hoped it was.

I am thinking of a good way to get back inside and enjoy the rest of the concert when red and blue lights start flashing down the street. This venue gets a lot of noise complaints. Some of the cops might even be the same ones that busted Christopher's house earlier this week for a noise complaint, and that will be a pain in the ass. I'm thinking about going around the side of the building to tell Eric that if he's smoking weed he should probably ditch it when out of the second cop car that pulls up steps a guy in a suit. The Man. When I see him I get the power of flight and use it to get around the side of the building before Christine even knows I'm gone.

Eric seems to know why I'm tear-assing toward him and his semi-circle of weed smokers and without thinking about it he starts booking in the same direction three steps ahead of me. The smokers follow suit, thinking they know why we're running and figuring they ought to too. I guess they're right, there are cops here and for them the consequences of being caught in public with a joint and whatever else they have in their pockets might include spending the night at the police station, an embarrassing call to their parents if they're in high school, a misdemeanor charge if they're not. But their lives will continue and they'll get to keep going to shows. Eric and I, who knows, but if we keep running and don't stop and don't get tripped up at least we get another day of running.

And we do keep running, really pretty good at it now, and the smokers break off after what they figure is a reasonably safe distance from the cops, and we must look incredibly paranoid to keep sprinting with nobody in blue chasing us. But we keep looking behind us and seeing The Man, always coming around the corner no matter how fast we run. Downtown is pretty barren tonight since there are no sporting events, and our feet are loud as shit among the skyscrapers. Eric's breathing is loud too, raggedy, I guess maybe from smoking, but on top of that something sounds broken. He keeps running, though. I think like that Dance Dance Revolution game, we're both waiting for the other to stop.

By the time we seem to have lost The Man we're in what I guess you would call the barrio. I throw my hood up and sit in a bus shelter with a broken light.

Eric takes out his phone.

"It could be tapped," I say.

Eric nods like, of course, then crosses the street and calls Christopher from a pay phone. Christopher is, I imagine, still at the show or maybe in the back of a paddywagon or maybe having his nuts shocked by mysterious government agents in order to get him to surrender our location, so Eric leaves a voicemail, something along the lines of we're sorry we got them mixed up in our mess, we never meant to drag them down with us. It sounds overdramatic but we haven't been home or at school in almost a week and we're fugitives from some cipher with whole stores of really good drugs and we're feeling pretty overdramatic, if you want to know the truth.

We walk south down side streets parallel to Central Avenue, not wanting to actually go down the well-lit main street.

"I used to have T-ball down here," I say.

"Oh yeah?" Eric says. "Were you good?"

"No," I say, "terrible."

Come to think of it the aluminum bat I had for T-ball got thrown in my brother's trunk the night he and his friends were supposed to take care of our problem. I am sort of disgusted that something from my childhood was almost used to bludgeon somebody, but then I think how if it actually had been used to bludgeon somebody, I might be home in bed instead of walking down side streets parallel to Central Avenue, and Eric might be home, not in bed, listening to early music on the NPR affiliate or thinking about fractals. I feel a weird mix of emotions, none of which seem like they go together but they all get felt at the same time. I'm getting more of these lately.

Central terminates at the mountains. On the other side of the mountains is our neighborhood and lots of others. We hit a cul-de-sac and just keep walking. I remind myself that they're not even technically big enough to be mountains, they're really just hills we call "the mountains," but it's dark and past midnight and there could be coyotes and God knows what else up here, the homeless junkies who've been kicked out of their model homes, anything. But no one would think to look for us up here. So two unathletic boys stumble upwards in the middle of the night toward the big TV antennas with red lights on them that always meant home to me after coming back from vacation or summer camp.

"This is really scary," Eric says. I'm glad he thinks so, too.

When we get to the top of the mountains or the hills or what-ever they are, I am not surprised to see there are not actual TVs mounted on the antennas showing what they're broadcasting. It is too bad the red lights are serving their purpose of keeping planes from flying too low: if they were low enough we could grab on to their bellies and get away.

"What if we left?" I say to Eric. "Like, drove away, or flew? Went to California?"

"No," Eric says, right on top of me. "Running is just running. Let them come."

With our neighborhoods spread out below us, most everything dark except for the orange streetlights wrapped in strands around blocks with mansions and blocks with normal houses and blocks with no houses at all yet, Eric tells me we'd better just stand and fight.

"You don't have to if you don't want to," he says.

"Nah, I will. I will. But who are we fighting and what are we fighting them with?"

"I gotta show you something," Eric says, and starts down the hill towards home.

It's faster going downhill and by the time we get to the bottom the cuffs of my jeans are full of stickers and cactus needles. Nothing has stuck itself straight up into my shoe yet, which is good, but I'm looking forward to walking on pavement again at the bottom of the hill. There's a fence and on the other side of it are construction sites that become neighborhoods farther along. We hop the fence and Eric veers right, towards more desert. We're heading away from the hills, walking alongside civilization, houses on our left and more desert on our right.

There used to be desert behind my house, then they threw a band of highway a mile or two away in the desert and filled that space with houses, and that's where Eric's house is. Someday they'll throw a highway to our right and fill the space we're in now with houses. It's just starting to get light on the very edge of the sky by the time we get to where I guess we're going, which is the desert that's behind Eric's house right now and won't be anymore some-day. I followed him out here one day and caught him looking like Lord of the Flies. I know sort of where we are because of the fast-food signs I can see from here, the Sonic and the Wendy's and the Exxon that go together near the freeway. My head does that thing where you had no idea where you were and everything's a strange blur but then you see a landmark and that orients you and sud-denly you can fit everything in your head.

Eric stops, looks around. "We can rest here for a while until it gets light." He lies down with his back against something big and artificial, a dug-up drainpipe or something. I lean back against it as well and start trying to pick stickers and burrs out of my jeans but it's dark and I can't really see and I keep pricking myself, so after a while I just lay my head back and fall asleep.

Later the sun's up almost completely and I sort of forget where I am and I really want to get the sun out of my eyes so I turn my head to the left. There's some graffiti or something on the drainpipe near my shoulder. It's this elaborate, bent fleur-de-lis: the banner of the Thragnacian Sentinels, who are charged with keeping a baby wormhole from devouring the universe in *TimeBlaze*. I didn't know Eric did graffiti. But the symbol is kind of way too good and intricate to be graffiti. I think I must still be asleep but I'm pretty sure it's broad daylight two miles out of town and I am dozing with my back against a Thragnacian Containment Pylon.

I stand up and turn around and the thing is so white in the sun my eyes hurt from looking at it. The pylon isn't floating at a point in space emitting an invisible antimatter field that, in concert with all the other pylons, keeps the wormhole from tearing up more of the universe's fabric, and even weirder, it isn't sitting all flat and miniature and two-dimensional on a drawing pad on my desk, it's out here full-size, inactive, and buried halfway in the sand. All its curves, all its insignia, all the design details I cribbed from the cover of a copy of Ray Bradbury's *The Martian Chronicles* I got from the school library, they're all here two miles from my house in the real world with breathing people and cars.

Beyond the pylon, farther into the desert, Eric is peeing behind a bush. When he turns around he sees me see the thing and the first thing I ask him is "How did you build it?"

"I didn't," he says, "I sort of thought it. I thought it."

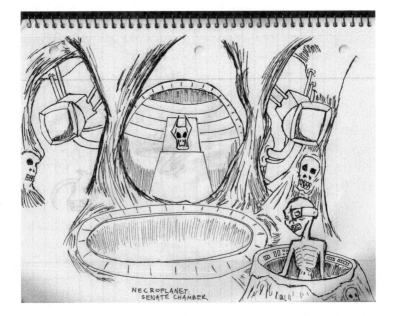

NECROPLANET:
SENATE CHAMBER

//

"On your bad days."

"Yeah. For a long time, they were just. Well, bad. Really painful and I would sweat and hallucinate. It was like an awful fever or what Jesse told me a bad acid trip was like." Jesse is one of the college kids we'll probably never see again after getting them busted. "But the hallucinations were extraordinarily vivid, I couldn't differentiate between what was real and what wasn't. And that was scary, so I locked myself in my room, and, I guess, risked freaking out and jumping out the window like in an antidrug commercial but other than that I was reasonably okay. I put everything remotely dangerous in my closet or the garage so I wouldn't hang myself with anything or swing on any hallucinations with something sharp and accidentally gouge myself."

"I saw you in the middle of one of those."

"You did. At least, I remember you. It's kind of . . . hard to tell. Anyway, the hallucinations, after we started working on *TimeBlaze* they were almost exclusively derived from that. Characters, settings, monsters. The monsters were the worst. One time it was The Man. And I don't remember exactly what was happening, but we were fighting, and I knocked his sunglasses off. They went flying into some corner of my room, and he went away, everything went away, I came out of it, I didn't think about it again, and then I was digging in that corner for a record or something a week later and they were there. The sunglasses."

"Hmmm," I say. Because what you say when your best friend tells you things in his mind, things the two of you thought up together, those things get real at some point inexplicably, what you say is, "Hmmm."

"That was the first thing that, I don't know, appeared, became real, something. Generated."

"Can you control it?"

"I don't know. I read this novel once where this character was having a dream and afterwards he couldn't tell if he had been controlling the dream or what. I mean, obviously it's all coming from me, so on some level, subconsciously . . . I don't know," Eric says, rapping his knuckles on the pylon, the whole thing resonating with this otherwordly metallic sound. "When it happens I don't know what's real, what isn't. I'm insane."

"Isn't part of being insane thinking things that aren't real are real? People who kill their kids because they hear God's voice, see visions, stuff like that?"

"Right, that's what I'm saying."

"What you're telling me is, some of those things that aren't real that you think are when you're like this, they become real."

"Right."

"So you're not insane at all, then."

Eric laughs. He uses one of the pylon's gunwales to pick himself up off the ground. He dusts off his jeans.

"It was kind of sad. It appeared like this, buried. It was working for a couple seconds, you should've seen it, it was pretty incredible. Its stabilization afterburners were firing these blue flames and I was concerned it was going to hit a cactus and start a brushfire or something. But then it sputtered out and died and after everything else in the dream or whatever you want to call it was over, it was still here."

"Do you still have the glasses?"

Eric tramps into the brush a few feet, and pulls out a dirty black trashbag. He shakes the dust off of it, reaches in, and pulls out a completely normal-looking pair of black Ray-Ban sunglasses. He tramps back over to the pylon and hands them to me. Not only do they look totally normal, they're a little busted, probably from being in the middle of the desert and maybe from this fight Eric says he had.

I hold them up like I'm going to put them on. When they're a few inches from my nose, this sort of golden cloud appears between my eyes and the lenses. As they get closer and closer to my face, the cloud snaps into focus. It becomes a dancing collection of goldenrod yellow letters and numbers, all of them corresponding to and crowded around anything I can see: the bushes, the trees, the mountain, Eric. The pylon in particular swarms with information. I can't read any of this information, of course, because it's all in High Yewuan, the ancient language of the technological priesthood that were the forebearers to the Committee, and even if it were in English I'd have a hard time understanding it, because it's coming at such a fast clip. The Man, whose every brainwave is trained and geared toward his mission, it just washes over him. He gets what he needs.

"Dude," I say.

"I know," Eric says.

"So these . . ." I take them off because I'm starting to get a headache already. "And the pylon?"

Eric doesn't say anything. He turns and walks away from our town, into the desert. I follow him. He scrambles down a little hill and turns. Carved out of the hill is what you'd call a cave, if you called the hills we walked down "mountains," it's really more of a hole in a dirt mound but it's more cave than I'm used to. I follow him in out of the sun and it takes a second for my eyes to focus and before they do I'm ready for anything, prepped to have anything from my imagination ripped out and splattered on the actual world, ready to see a buzzing underground wasp-city or row upon row of Neanderthal clones in glowing orange jars, but instead I see dirt walls and something under a dirty blue tarp. There's blood everywhere. Dried onto the walls of the dirt hole and dried on the floor after oozing out from underneath the tarp. I think, oh my God, somebody stumbled upon Eric while he was out here in the midst of his thing and they didn't have the sense, weren't enough of a friend to him to run when he told them to run, and he killed them. Wittingly or unwittingly, sane or insane, and now I'm going to have to help him bury whoever's under the tarp.

Eric reaches down and pulls the tarp back and instead of the body of a ten-year-old skate punk or Mexican migrant worker, it's a dog. A dog with horns, but still a dog. A Yerum Battlebeast to the people of the Argot Cluster, but still a dog, a really weird dog, to anyone who isn't me and Eric, the people who came up with it.

"Holy shit dude," I say, "holy fucking shit."

You can tell Eric is weirded out by me crying. Hell, I'm weirded out by me crying.

"It attacked me," he says, "I had to. But you should've seen it before. It was amazing. We did a really good job."

But it isn't that it's dead, I'm not crying about a dog from a made-up galaxy that probably has no business existing anyway, it's not any of that, it's, I don't know, I had sort of just started dealing with the fact that Eric meant anything is possible, because if he is able to exist, imagine what else could exist out there, imagine what else could be coming true. But what the sunglasses and the pylon half-buried in the dirt and the dead dog at my feet, the dog with the skin just as rough as I shaded it on a piece of notebook paper on some afternoon last November, what these things mean is that he's not only a signifier that anything can be real, he's the thing that makes them real. And that fucks me up so completely, makes me so crazy happy that I have to cry and like any teenage boy I'm proud for almost never crying but now I'm even more proud because I saved it for this, this is a moment that deserves it. I wish I hadn't cried about a girl a couple of months ago so I'd have more tears for this moment, this moment that rips up the term *reality*, forever un-marries it from the word *boring*. I am also, I have to admit, terrified, because I have always lived in this one world, and I am leaving it, right now in this moment, for a whole different one. I imagine it's a lot how leaving for college feels, if you were going to college in Atlantis.

But I can't tell Eric that right this second, I don't even know it well enough to say it and I barely know it well enough now. What I end up saying is, "How did you kill it?"

"My dad's gun," Eric says, and moves aside a rock to reveal a handgun in the dirt.

I put the sunglasses back on, even though we're in the shade, even though it means being showered with a whole lot of arcane symbols that I designed but don't know the meaning of. I guess it's uncomfortable to me, having my eyes out there, unprotected, with tears streaming out of them that I can't do anything to stop. The glasses were a by-product of the fact that I'm not great at drawing eyes, that I could get nine tenths of the way through a really successful depiction of some character and then have it ruined by the delicate balance that eyes are, the way we have so much deep unconscious experience with them that when an artist has done a shitty job of striking that balance we look at them and the whole thing feels wrong. And now here they are on my face, here they are collecting my tears.

They have the unintended side effect of making the whole world look like a video game: one of the only things on the projected HUD (heads-up display) that I can actually make sense of is the status bars. It scans every living thing in your field of vision and tells you how healthy they are, how close to death. Every animal, anyway, or artificial construct that's close enough to an animal. This is useful to The Man when he is fighting somebody and he needs to know how many more bullets it will take to bring them down, or when he's presented with a dying alien and he needs to know how much longer he has to get whatever information he needs from the creature before it expires completely. Terrestrial plants get a pass, which is a good thing, too, or the desert would be a forest of green, yellow, and red status bars. It's interesting to me because I look at Eric and see that his status bar is yellow, less than half full, meaning he's closer to dying than not.

"When's your next bad day?" I ask.

"Hard to say," Eric says. "They're happening closer together now."

"That's not gonna be good enough," I say. "We can't afford to wait for it, and we can't afford it being erratic when it happens. You need to be able to control when it happens, and what we get out of it when it does."

"Okay," says Eric.

And in case you were wondering, I don't know what I'm talking about. But my friend the alien is dying and the forces arrayed against us are closing in and it's time to make moves.

And in case you were wondering, the handgun in the dirt is the gun they said he had on him when everything happened.

The rest of the day is me teaching Eric to be the best world-busting genetic anomaly he can be. It's basically Yoda teaching Luke how to use the Force if Yoda didn't know anything about the Force and couldn't use it himself.

"So here's the thing," I say when I have stopped crying and removed the sunglasses and emerged into the sun feeling like our suburb's teenage General Patton. "What does he really have, right? The guy who's chasing us. We think he might be part of some vast government conspiracy. There's also a chance he's just some guy from, like, an evil pharmaceutical giant and he's bribed his way into the cops working for him. But that's it. He has cops, and cops have guns and authority. But what we have—what you have . . . is a power."

Eric looks down at the ground.

"It is, man. It just is. There's no arguing that anymore. We just have to like, figure out how you can control it."

"I can't."

"You can't yet. I may not have thought as much about this thing of yours as you have, but if all you've thought is 'Screw it, I can't,' then all that thought was wasted. I just found out about this and I'm telling you you can. I don't know that you can, but I'm telling you you can, because you have to."

Sometimes the best thing you can do for someone is not let them apologize for how special they are, to pass themselves off as mediocre. When Christine and I were together she never stopped telling me how good my drawings were. She wasn't sold on the subject matter and she thought I should spend more time in my "legit drawing" sketchbook, but she never let me cop to merely doodling. And even after all the shit we've been through I still feel a little cooler because of it. Eric is like me, obsessed with mutations and powers, so getting him excited about what he is should not be hard.

"So it's like, an accumulation of not sleeping. Like, whatever it is normal people get rid of when they sleep, you don't get rid of it. Or, whatever it is that enables you to not sleep, the side effect of an accumulation of that thing is, this. The bad days."

"Right."

"So the question is, how do we speed up that accumulation? How do we get you to sleep less than you already are?"

We slip back in from the desert. We go to the grocery store and buy a really ridiculous amount of energy drinks because the thought is, overstimulating Eric will tire him out quicker. Like, when I drink a bunch of Red Bull to stay up all night playing first-person shooters on Xbox, I am extraordinarily wired for a short period of time and then suddenly bone-tired, more tired than I would have been had I never drunk all that stuff in the first place. And after we go to the store we go to my house to steal my brother's Adderall, because for someone who doesn't have attention deficit disorder, like Eric (who probably has way too much attention, if anything), it is apparently an incredible stimulant. And we are getting enough energy drinks for both of us to have way too many energy drinks, and we are going to get enough Adderall for both of us, because all this stuff he's going to do to try and affect his brain chemistry, I am going to do as well, even though I don't have the same brain chemistry as him at all and it will probably just make me momentarily super-stimulated and then shortly afterward very exhausted. And I'm going to do it because before we reenter society to go to the grocery store and my house, we have this conversation:

"Okay. But you have to do it, too."

"Like the roofies? C'mon, man, why is it I have to do everything WITH you? Like when they're testing lab rats, scientists don't cut their own brains open as well, you know what I mean?"

"I'm a lab rat?"

"No! But you get what I'm saying. It was one thing when it was just us, but now there's someone after us, and maybe it would make sense to have one of us fully lucid while the other one's—"

Eric looks down and spits in the dirt and I stop. I don't even have that big of a problem with it. It's only like twice as much energy drink as I've ever had in me before (again, late-night Xbox FPS sessions—you decide you need to be the most stimulated when you really don't need to be at all). And I've never taken Adderall, which people take recreationally as a drug, so that'll be another milestone I will have conquered in my un-rewritable high school experience. There is so much in this world Eric can only experience alone because of who and what he is—so much he's had to do alone, that I guess basically what he's saying when he says "you have to do it too" is, *I want somebody to come with me as far as they possibly can.*

We put the gun back in its hiding place and cover the beast with the blue plastic tarp and put the sunglasses back in their black plastic trashbag and Eric places them where he left them, in the bushes, and the two of us walk back into town.

When we get to my house we have two shopping bags each full of cans of various ridiculous sizes and absurd colors. If this were just a random Saturday night I would stick with old reliable Red Bull but we are each going to have to drink a lot of the stuff and the exact same thing in quantities that big would definitely get old and probably increase the (still honestly pretty big) chance of one or both of us throwing up. So beyond Red Bull we also have your second-tier Monsters and Rock Stars and weird, possibly local junior varsity energy drinks like NUCLEAR WARTHOG (all capitals) and something called Lizard Juice, which advertises itself on the can as the official Energy Beverage of the American Pro Dirt-Biking Circuit.

It's ten thirty on a Friday morning, so no one is home. My house has that empty, on-a-school-day feel, like no one is supposed to be here. We put the drinks in the fridge for the moment and Eric follows me upstairs. In my brother's room, I open the third drawer down and peel back the blanket reading Phoenix Suns Western Conference Champions. Underneath it is way more drugs than there were when I hit him up for the date-rape drug, and they're all prescription bottles marked with the logo of Lunaspa-Albans. In addition to definitely putting Eric's life and probably mine in danger, my ratting out of Eric to these people seems to have had the consequence of making my older brother, who was a small-time low-stakes drug dealer and frequent but low-stakes drug user, into either a way bigger drug dealer, a way bigger drug user, or probably a hazy not very well thought-out but certainly more dangerous combination of both. I take the only bottle I recognize, his Adderall, remove four pills, put the cap back on, replace the bottle, and replace the blanket we got for Christmas when we were kids, and feel just awesome about myself. About the only thing I don't have to feel that guilty for is taking his ADD medication. He might very well have ADD but he doesn't take the pills himself, he mostly trades or sells them to kids who are also not taking them for the purposes of better focusing on their precalculus homework.

"I'm going to get some clothes out of my room," I say. "Do you want any?"

"No, that's okay," Eric says. "I should probably go by my house for a little while today anyway."

"Do you think that's safe?"

"It might not be but I really should." He says it with too much conviction for me to argue.

I change my shirt in my room, then I pack a couple of additional T-shirts into a backpack I haven't used since sixth grade. Before we leave I get on my dad's computer and I Google Lunaspa-Albans. Their website is well designed but remarkably barren and nonspecific. It's mostly pictures of multiracial women in goggles looking happily at test tubes, with a lot of slogans like "Providing Solutions for a Changing World." They claim to have offices in seven nations, with their main one in Reading, Pennsylvania. Rather than make me scared, their seeming bigness and mystery gives me mental images of me and Eric pulling up in front of their Reading headquarters in a stolen car, taking the fight to them. It's really unrealistic for two teenage boys with six hundred dollars in the world between them who've been truant for the past several school days, but not so much for two teenage boys, one who's a remarkable transcendent being and the other who's obsessed with pushing the first to discover the limits of his abilities. Like a lot of things that make me happy, I have to keep reminding myself about Eric's making things real, but when I remember, it chases all the lonely and scared and tired out of me. Eric comes out of the bathroom and in a ritual honed in late-night looking-at-Internet-porn sessions, I close out of the browser, open it back up, erase the cache of viewed websites, and we go downstairs and take our bags from the fridge.

"Do you still have any of the *TimeBlaze* art?" Eric says.

"Not really," I say, "it was all at your house." I don't mention the reason it's gone, the reason we're both well aware of, which is that Eric scattered it in front of my house and we only recovered that one page from the bush and everything else I never cleaned up out of spite, it was just gone, carried away by the wind.

"Right," he says. "Bring a notebook and some pencils."

We are going back to the desert together to try and get Eric to have one of his bad days. Hopefully, to have a hallucination that becomes real. And this time, instead of him telling me to go away and me going away, as fast as I can, hopefully avoiding his mom, he isn't going to ask me to go away and I'm not going to go away. Even if in some unexpected spasm of really bad hallucination he asks me to go away, I'm not going to go away.

We walk through the dusty alleys behind my house, switching paths erratically, taking the backstreets of the backstreets, which are actually just dirt paths filled with tumbleweeds and people's bulk trash. I think it's the tumbleweeds and the dirt, and the fact that we are walking side by side like Western lawmen on the way to the showdown, if instead of passing a flask of whiskey back and forth the lawmen were drinking fizzy yellow energy drinks with names like NUCLEAR WARTHOG, but I start to get pretty psyched on us and how cool we are. I kill the last already-flat sips of my third energy drink and drop the can at my feet.

Eric stops. He turns and walks back and picks the can up, then takes it over to somebody's dumpster and tosses it in.

"Don't litter," he says.

A couple minutes later and my heart is trying to get up enough speed to go back in time and we're coming out of the neighborhood to the edge of the desert, the new home for kids like us. I imagine this is how Agtranian Berserkers must feel right before they go into battle, with hearts the size of human heads pretty much bursting with superadrenaline. I think how neat it might be if I ever got to meet one. We could compare notes. The sun is right overhead, completing my Western showdown delusion. But this isn't the showdown, yet. This is just the training sequence.

By Eric's request, I draw a Tllnar Defender. It's hard for him to ask, because neither of us really knows how to say "Tllnar" because it looks cool and alien on the page but it's tough to say out loud with a human mouth. The Tllnar are cyborgs by birth, natural fusions of technology and flesh and it's hard to pinpoint what created what.

"As detailed as you can," Eric reminds me.

"Yup," I say, putting the finishing touches on the Defender's faceplate.

"I think I prefer Lizard Fuel to NUCLEAR WARTHOG, but neither of them stacks up to the more popular national brands. And I think that we can rest assured that none of them is the color they are when they're done being mixed. Nothing comes out of the industrial process the color it is by the time you consume it. Everything comes out gray. I saw a special on the History Channel." For the moment, we have the long-winded Eric back, thanks to energy drinks and ADD pills.

"Done," I say, tearing the sheet from the notebook and handing it to Eric. Tllnar Defenders are small, around three and a half feet, and this one only takes up half the page.

"Cool," Eric says. "I'm going to go off and study this. And probably pee a lot."

"Okay," I say.

"I'll be back," he says.

"Okay," I say. Eric wanders off into the brush, away from town.

My hand was shaky when I was drawing, and I wonder if, if and when it comes into existence, the Tllnar Defender's body will be all zigzagged and jittery, the way I accidentally drew it. I wonder if it will come into being piece by piece, slowly fading into our world, or there will be, like, a flash of blue light, or if it will literally spring out of Eric's forehead like he's Zeus giving birth to a new nymph or something. I wonder a lot of things really really fast, thanks to the caffeine and drugs. I have this image of my thoughts as football players bursting through a big piece of butcher paper as they come out of the tunnel at a pep rally, and then the players BECOME the paper, and more football-player thoughts burst through them, and on and on like that, while everybody cheers. I don't know how much time passes.

Someone yells. A war cry. Eric comes running out of the brush like something's chasing him. He turns and wheels on whatever it is once he reaches a clearing, but nothing ever comes. Still, he looks at a point in the dirt, like, that's my enemy. Suddenly he's knocked flat. His back hits the ground and he goes "WHUUF," the sound of having the wind knocked out of you. His arms and legs strain like there's something on top of him trying to push him off, but there isn't. It's like the world's most convincing bit of pantomime: the thing on top of him has weight and strength, it just doesn't have existence. It's tough to watch, and creepy to watch, but it isn't yet scary, because there's just nothing there.

Eric grunts, loud, and sits up, his arms in front of him like he just pushed the thing off with a lot of effort. Then his face jerks to the side and there's blood on it, like he was struck. Then, the thing that struck him is there. It just is. I blink and Eric is fighting a Tllnar Defender tooth and fucking nail.

If you've ever had something you've only ever previously seen in your head and on loose-leaf notebook pages just appear in front of you, you will sympathize with my first reaction, which is to be completely still. And if you've ever had that thing appear while trying to kill your best friend, and if you had a history of abandoning said friend when he was battling monsters both hallucinated and hallucinated-into-reality, then you will sympathize with my second reaction, which is to run screaming, literally screaming, at the little thing, and tackle it.

Eric has had us build a weakness into all our characters, and the Tllnar Defender's weakness is its optical array, basically its eyes if it were all biological instead of half-and-half. I grab a rock from

nearby and raise it high above my head and bring it down on the
Defender's face, or what would be its face, as hard as I can, cracking the V-shaped optical array down the middle. I bash it again,
shattering it completely. It stops grunting and squealing underneath me. Metallic claws and tubes and valves begin retracting in
on each other as the thing's tech superstructure compresses itself
into one tiny capsule that can be reclaimed by Tllnar Vultures
sweeping the battlefield. The capsule can then be brought back to
a lumbering, living Field Command Post, repaired, and reinjected
with flesh, in accordance with the shrewd Tllnar precept that metal
is expensive but meat is cheap. Or anyway, that's what would happen to the capsule if this Defender had died in battle on the per-
manent warfields of Perseid 8, but since it died being bludgeoned
by one of the human kids who made it up in the desert five minutes outside of an Arizona suburb, the capsule is probably just
going to sit there embedded in its dead body, and maybe glint in
the sun months or years from now when the wind uncovers it
where Eric and I are going to bury it in the desert.

I stand up and dust myself off. I look over at Eric.

"So that's why I said we should give them all a weakness, pretty
much," he says.

Even though it's small, the thing is heavy as hell. Eric and I carry it
some ways into the desert, find a natural depression in the ground,
and push as much dirt over it as we can. We don't do a very good
job, if you want to know the truth. But hiding it doesn't seem all
that important. And I think, *I really don't hope we keep bringing
things out of our imaginary world only to have to kill them.* And I
think, *Did Eric kill everything that ever came out of his head?* There's
no way, right? And maybe it's because in this moment I go from
buzzed to epically tired, after we've pushed the last bit of dirt into
place, but I think of the weird Martian red cloud floating overhead
when it wasn't even monsoon season, and I think of the thing my
dad hit with his SUV on the way back from San Diego that left a

big yellow stain then disappeared into the night, and I think of everybody's cars, the parking-lot graveyard, as though some Altra-Troops hit them with an EMP. Everything becomes clear, or rather, remarkably unclear. Whereas before, I was sure the world made some sort of lame sense, I just hadn't figured it out. Now I know I won't ever know.

The mound of dirt vibrates a little as the superstructure finishes its capsuling sequence. I need a nap really badly.

"How come it's always a fight?" I say to Eric as we walk back to our staging area. "How come nothing ever appears and gives you a high-five?"

"I don't know," Eric says, "but it helps that it always feels right. I mean, when I go into it . . . when it starts. My mind kind of shifts, and I belong there. Consciously I know I'm imagining it, but on some level I just feel a part of the story."

"Cool," I say.

"Something I've been worried about. . . . Am I going to break the world?" Eric says.

"I don't think so," I say.

"Because I'm really worried I might break the world."

"You think pretty highly of yourself," I say. Eric laughs.

"You should go home," he says. "We both should. One night can't hurt. And if he shows up at either of our houses, we take to the back alleys and call the other person, and we improvise."

"Are you sure?"

"I have to go home tonight," he says.

"Okay," I say.

Eric looks right into the sun and squints and says, "I'm not tired. Want to go see a movie?"

We dust ourselves off and take the bus to the movie theater and see a zombie movie we never would have proposed going to see with any of the college kids. They are probably too cool and adult for it. I think about how when I was at that movie with Eric and

Christine I desperately wanted zombies to burst into the edges of the frame and rip some dude's heart out. I think of that movie as the world and Eric's thing as zombies bursting in. Except it doesn't have to be zombies. It could be literally anything.

We take the bus back and talk in hushed tones, finalizing details. Tomorrow morning behind Eric's house by the Thragnacian Containment Pylon, we will make our last stand. Eric gets up to get off before me.

"See you tomorrow," he says.

"See you tomorrow," I say.

I let myself into my house. Nobody's home yet. I go up to my room, and halfway up the stairs, every ounce of strength leaves me and I just barely make it to bed and when I do I crash, hard. And the last clear thing I think before I do (and granted I think it really fast, my inner monologue is still like a cartoon chipmunk having a panic attack) is, Eric can't crash. The poor kid has to live through everything.

I wake up later when my dad knocks on my door and says dinner is ready. He cooked tonight, stir-fry. It isn't half bad and my brother and me and my dad all eat around the kitchen table and no one is mean to anyone. My dad asks me how the trip was and I say "It was cool. I'm exhausted."

After dinner I go upstairs and lie down on my bed. A star explodes in my chest and sends millions of feelings in every direction. I pick up my phone and call Christine. She picks up after two rings.

"Hello?" she says.

"Hey," I say. "Just so you know, I love you and I'm not mad at you. And everything's going to be okay."

"What's going on?" Christine says.

"Nothing," I say. "Everything's fine."

I hang up the phone and fall asleep.

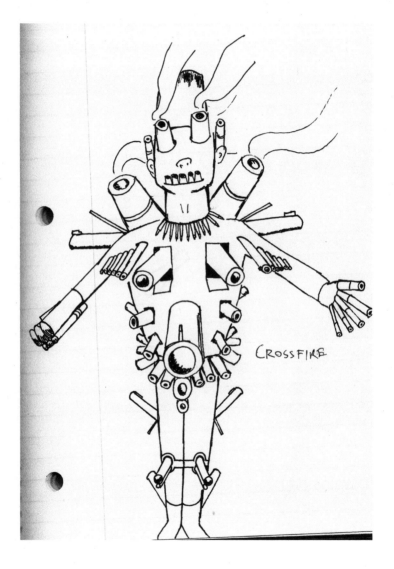

CROSSFIRE

The next morning, it happens like this: I call The Man and say, "I'm tired of running. Do you want to know where my friend is?"

"The last time I received a call of this nature," The Man says, "it was a trap, if you'll remember. I was threatened by some teenagers whom I had to buy off."

"It's not a trap."

"Just be decent and let me know if I need to restock."

"It's not a trap. I just want everything to go back to the way it was." Which is kind of true. More accurately, I want everything to go back to the way it was except now I'm friends with a kid who can make anything real. I want to go back to school like that. I want to own the place.

"Where is he now?"

"He'll be at the—"

"No. No meetings. Not where he will be, only where he is. Right now."

"Home. He's at his house. As far as I know he's at his house."

"Alright. If this all works out you will be amply rewarded."

"I just want you to leave me alone."

"If this all works out I'll be out of your way and you'll be rewarded. It won't take much on your part. Just silence."

"Okay. What are you going to do to him?"

"He won't be harmed." The Man hangs up.

I call Eric and tell him we're going ahead with the plan early and he should head out behind the house, to the hole in the dirt, to the pylon, our staging area, and I'll be there as soon as I can.

Stealing my brother's car and the rest of his medication involves going into his room, where he's still asleep with his arm wrapped around some girl whose hip bones are tent-poling her underwear, she's that skinny, and taking his keys out of his jeans on the floor. When I have them almost worked out of the pocket one of the keys clanks against his studded belt and he stirs but he doesn't wake up. The girl opens her eyes. She stares at me. I freeze and open my mouth to start to explain. But she closes her eyes again, like she was never fully awake. My brother and this girl seem to be violating what he once told me was one of the "Ten Crack Commandments," which is to never get high on your own supply. I guess he figures if it's not crack, it's okay. It's like ten a.m. I guess they're not going to school today. Since they're almost comatose I get way less concerned about noise and root through his drug drawer. I take the whole bottle of Adderall and go downstairs.

I don't really actually know how to drive, but the bus is going to be too slow and if careening around the suburbs is the most dangerous thing I do today I'll be lucky. I teach myself how to do a rolling stop and I make Eric's neighborhood in five minutes and I don't fender-bend anybody.

There are no cars in front of Eric's house, and no helicopters hovering overhead, and no SWAT teams coming up from the storm drains. I roll up the driveway and hop out, cut through the backyard and hop the fence.

Trudging through the dirt I think maybe I'm going the wrong way because I get to around where the pylon should appear between the cacti and the scrub brush, but it isn't where it should be. There's a big mound of dirt, though. Eric covered it up. It's just a little hill and maybe it will be forever but probably just until they start building houses here. Maybe it will get uncovered by the wind along with the Tllnar Defender and my brother will come out here and shoot it with paintballs when the semiconscious hip-bones girl breaks up with him.

"Dude! It's me!" Nobody comes out of the dirt hole. I jump down and there's nobody in there. The tarp is gone, and the Yerum Battlebeast.

"Darren?" I look up and standing at the mouth of the hole is Eric's mom. "What are you doing here?"

"Uhm. Looking for Eric." Talking to moms is never not hard, especially when you're not pretending to be someone else, and I'm out of practice. "You wouldn't happen to know where he is, would you?"

"He went to school," she says, mystified because it's a Wednesday and of course he's in school. Except he's not supposed to be in school, he's supposed to be back here with me getting ready for the showdown. "How was your college experience?"

"What? Oh. It was good. It was really interesting. I think I'm probably gonna go there. You know? Or, uhm. Or NAU."

"Well, Eric would sure miss you. If you're going by school, bring him his backpack." She holds out Eric's red bag. "He forgot it. He can be such a space cadet sometimes."

I take Eric's bag. "Have a nice day," she says, and she walks back toward the house. It makes me really sad to see her go for some reason, and I have this overwhelming desire to be normal. To give it all back in exchange for being allowed to be normal, even more normal than I was before this whole thing started. It makes sense for me then why Eric needed to go home. Maybe I'll have him generate me a mom. But right now the sun is moving across the sky and the plan is already going haywire and my friend needs me.

The rock is still over in one corner of the hole, and underneath it is Eric's dad's gun. I unzip the bag, put the gun inside, put the backpack on my back and rolling-stop my way to our high school.

My brother has a parking space and even though parking is a concern for me the two spaces next to his are empty as well, so I don't clip anybody. He and Jake and Alan all got parking spots together. I guess they aren't coming to school today either.

It's the very end of second period and I catch Eric coming out his class, no backpack and empty-eyed.

"What's going on, man? What happened to behind the house? Our final stand?"

"I went back there and, I don't know, it's too empty back there. If he comes for me and he takes me there's no one to notice. But here, we've got a whole audience."

"Right, and he'll probably just hold off until you leave. I thought the whole point was to lure him in so we could fight him off once and for all. And the reason he can't come and take you here is the same reason you can't end him here."

"Huh," he says, "I guess you're right."

"Do you want your bag? You look pretty conspicuous without it."

"Uhm . . ."

"It's got your dad's . . . uhm . . . thing in it. I figured . . ."

"Oh, in that case, hold on to it. In a minute I'm not gonna be somebody you want handling a firearm."

"Dude! Don't say firearm in the middle of . . ." The reality sort of dawns on me, being in school with somebody else's backpack with somebody else's gun. I'm glad we don't go to an inner-city school with metal detectors. I think about how I've gotten to the point that Carl Whiteman with his list of kids who "deserved it" could only have angry revenge-fueled daydreams about getting to. Standing in the hallway during passing period, secretly tooled up.

We're both going to class as usual, and I guess just on instinct we end up out by the auditorium ramp at lunchtime, although neither of us has a lunch or really any desire to eat.

"Maybe it won't go down today," I say, "maybe he won't come."

"My mom told you I went to school?"

"Yeah. She was really nice to me."

"Last night she said it reflected well on you, that you would go to this honors college program. She told you. If he shows up she'll definitely tell him. She thinks he's from college."

"Yeah," I say. "How come it's taking so long?"

"Marshaling his forces," Eric says. The sun beats down on us. I guess it's almost spring.

"I'm really fucking sorry, man," I say. "This whole fucking thing is my fault. I told somebody in the first place and then when I had the chance I turned you in over some fucking girl."

"It's not your fault," Eric says. "I told somebody first. And anyway, I think it is my fault because I think I accidentally created him."

"Who?"

"The guy. The Man. We thought him up and I think I brought him into being. That day in my room. If the glasses can be real, he can too."

"Does he look like this guy?"

"A little. Not really. I dunno. It's pretty egotistical to think I made him, I guess, huh?"

"We did make him. In a way. Or I did. I called him. I'm sorry."

"Yeah. But if we made him, that means we can undo him," Eric says, washing an Adderall down with ginger ale.

It doesn't start like the Altratroops invading the school in *Time-Blaze*. All that happens is a cop car pulls up by the flagpole. No siren or anything. Two cops get out, normal fat cops who bust kids for skating. I think one of them might have been my DARE officer even. But then another police car pulls up, and another one, and another one. Slow as can be, a little army of cops shows up in front of the school. Their radios buzzing, all looking at each other like "It's a living." And I know they're not all inhuman monsters because the one who's driving the car The Man gets out of gives The Man a look like "Who is this asshole?" But it looks like he's in charge, and they all take orders from him because someone has told them to.

Eric doesn't freak out. I think I say "shit" and I can feel the backpack on my back and I can feel the gun inside of it screaming out prison time, screaming "shot on school premises." The garage door starts to open. I look back and see Eric at the controls.

"Let's go," says Eric, "this is as good a place as any," sounding all kinds of adult.

We get up and as we do I see a rock drop out of nowhere onto the concrete, making a loud crack. The Man and the cops hear it and turn to see their two soft targets walking into the drama department.

In the couple of months Christine and I went out I never made it back here. Whenever she'd talk about something that had happened that day in rehearsal or at a Theater Division meeting I'd imagine everything looking like the grainy video of clips from their plays being shown once a month on the school newscast. Kids in half-assed costumes, clownish in makeup, their "flats," as we learned they were called that one day out on the loading dock, being dwarfed by the size of the stage itself. It was a little hard to respect. But right now this seems like the ideal place for our purposes: as dark and expansive as the rest of the school is narrow and too well lit.

"I don't really know how to use this gun, man."

"You won't have to," Eric says, and pulls on one of the curtain ropes. The curtain comes up and instead of revealing a plywood-and-tempera-paint New York, underneath the curtain is a mech.

If you are a kid of a certain age and male you will know what I mean. A giant metal exoskeleton, like Voltron, like Battletech. Like *TimeBlaze,* because someday if we make it out of this alive people will read it and totally give us credit for changing the whole interpretation of mechs in sci-fi. The thing about mechs is, they're fucking, badass. The thing that's different about ours is, they're more badass.

I am good at drawing, I think. I am fucking good. Look at how cool this thing is, how well designed, how imaginative. I holler with joy and swing up into the cockpit. The thing is about three of me tall and one of me wide. I slide right in and the cockpit conforms to my body and the HUD slides over my face and I am home, this is perfect, this is incredible. I look down at Eric.

Eric: "That works, right?"

By way of response I rocket across the auditorium, a jet-propelled leap that's just graceful as hell, and I crush some seats but I do it beautifully.

"How long have you been hiding this in here?" The mech amplifies my voice to this metallic screech that would hurt my ears if I weren't in the cockpit.

"Since this morning," Eric said. "I came in early. If I ever have to drink another energy drink again, I think I'll kill myself."

"It'll be worth it," I say.

"Yup," Eric says, and at that moment I'm fine, I'm in a mech and everything I ever wanted to be real can be and we are unstoppable and Eric's thing means we'll be around forever, we'll be fine, and we will be.

I turn around to make sure there's no one else in the auditorium because I want to fire a rocket-propelled grenade but I don't want to hit anybody and when I turn back Eric is a ball of blue flame because suddenly he always has been. And just in time too, because the law is here. In the dim light of the stage are three cops, then five, then probably all the cops in our suburb.

"Drop it, assholes!" Drop what? The gun is in a backpack lying on the stage, and they can't know that, a backpack is normal in a school, a backpack makes sense, not a kid in a mech or a kid who's a glowing avatar. "Step out of the impossible vehicle" might make sense. Or "Extinguish yourself."

I make another leap for the stage and all of the sudden it's on: guns are out and blazing, cops who've never pulled a piece before in their lives are unloading rounds here in the auditorium of the school some of their kids probably attend. Maybe Tony DiAvalo's dad is here, I think he might be a cop. Hey, Mr. DiAvalo, look what I can draw. Fuck your son and his hustling M&Ms.

The rounds go ricocheting off the mech, we designed it to be bomb-proof so bullets are nothing, bullets are from this world and this thing is from beyond the stars, and I keep advancing on this one cop and he keeps firing right at the blast shield I can see through, and one bullet, I don't know how, one bullet bounces straight back and he catches a round in the hand and his gun blows up, classic. His hands are bleeding and I pick him up with the mech's mechanical arm and hold him out over the orchestra pit.

"Let us go," I screech mechanically.

The guy twists around in my mech's hand and stares directly into the blast shield. I don't think he can see me, but there is a look on his face of absolute un-cop-like shit-scaredness, and it bugs me that he is human. That he did not ask for this. That for all its video-game aspects this is not a video game.

"Stand down!" someone screams, and it's The Man. He comes out from behind a piece of stage furniture. "Stand down."

The cops put their guns away and I put the cop down on the stage. The Man was ducking. He's nothing we have to worry about. If Eric had created him, if he were what we made him, he would've dodged bullets and come for us like it was no big deal; our Man wouldn't need fat suburban cops. There's us and there's them now, and we're something else entirely.

"No need for this," The Man says, "no need," and comes out from behind the end table. Then, while I'm listening to The Man say something about how we can work this whole thing out, Eric screams.

"STOP!"

But it's too late. The bloody-handed cop has his gun out in his good hand and he fires into the vent on the mech that is its us-given weakness, the little one right below the blast shield and to the left of its gyrostabilizer. The whole thing powers down at once, the blast shield pops open, and Eric turns to see what the fuck is going on. In that second, The Man pulls something from his coat and stabs Eric in the neck with it. Eric's a kid again in that instant, no more blue flame, and the mech is no more and I'm down on the floor with the cop who just shot the vent, and I see that the thing the guy has driven into Eric's neck is a needle, the plunger totally depressed.

Eric is getting woozy. His eyes are starting to roll back in his head, and that's when he starts running. He starts running, his limbs puppet-y like he's drunk, like he's back in the IHOP parking lot. Tranquilizer in the veins of someone who can't be totally tranquilized.

God bless him but he goes and the Man runs after him, grabs him by the waist. Eric flails and fights and it's no use and I think, just go to sleep. Goddamnit, go to sleep. You did everything you could have done.

"What the fuck," says the cop with the bloody hands. "What the fucking fuck." The other cops must be thinking the same thing because I have enough time to roll over and unzip Eric's bag and train Eric's dad's gun on The Man, who is still holding a half-dead, drunk-looking exhausted Eric.

"Put him down."

"You can't get out of this," The Man says, and there's a loud echoing click of fifteen suburban cops pointing their weapons at me, just a kid with a gun, no more mech and maybe there never was.

"I know. But just put him down."

The Man does so, his hand still on Eric's collar so he can't go anywhere.

"There."

"Drop it, fuckwad!" one of the cops screams, and now I have something to drop so I do, and I'm still alive because I do what they say.

The cops walk me to a police car in handcuffs and The Man walks Eric to a black van with tinted windows and they don't need handcuffs, his legs are too heavy to run, heavy with what would put you and me in a coma but him it just slows him down.

When the van doors close that's the last time I see him.

14

My dad puts it best when he says he never thought I would be the kid to end up in jail.

But jail is what I end up in. Jail is distinct from prison, which is something I learn that I never knew before. Jail is where you are when you're awaiting trial. Prison is where you go after you've been convicted.

I can't believe myself in jail. I don't buy that I'm there. I also can't believe how much like a school it is, and I don't mean that to make some point about public education being indistinguishable from incarceration or whatever, I mean the architectural philosophies and materials that were used to build this jail are similar to the ones used to build my high school. I go to a fairly modern, antiseptic school and this is a fairly modern, antiseptic prison. The doors are the same, down to the little rectangular windows with the wire mesh inside, except they lock from the other side.

If I am quiet and introverted in a classroom full of students who don't care about me one way or the other, then here I am . . . I don't know. Operating under the principle that if we don't see other people they aren't there, I never look up, in holding, in the common areas, in the cafeteria, in the cell I share with a kid named Ricky. I don't meet anyone's eyes, ever. I see my own eyes reflected up at me from the pool of water forming underneath me in the shower.

In third grade I was convinced a classroom full of relatively well adjusted fourth-graders would suddenly jump me at any moment for no reason, even though they'd expressed no violent intentions. Here, everyone expresses their violent intentions towards you all the time, then retracts them, then laughs, then high-fives somebody, then reiterates the threat. Christine's college friends could sound ironic while meaning what they said. These kids can sound threatening and friendly all at once, and be both. It's always a joke, and not a joke, and a threat, and not a threat, but still a threat. You can put your head down and not look anyone in the eye but you can't not hear what gets yelled.

My third night after lights out when I can hear Ricky stumbling around in the dark trying to find our toilet, or at least I hope that's what he's doing, I realize I have been too dazed and scared to think for more than ten seconds about Eric and about what happened. And the next day I am just settled in enough to the terrifying routine that I am able to think about it, and I think about it for the next three days.

The difference between prison and jail isn't the only thing I learn. I learn that paralegals are not lawyers, and that Ricky would have tried harder to stay out of trouble if he'd known that, because his stepmom is a paralegal and he figured even if he got caught he'd be fine because she could get him off, so he's at the very least going to slap his stepmom when he gets out of here for giving him a mistaken impression. I learn that Corrections Officer Cliff Hines is particularly disappointed to see white kids like me in here with, in his words, "the niggers and the cholos." I learn a good deal of Spanish swear words, and am a few days and a few catcalls away from matching all the words to their definitions when I realize I've been in here a full week without seeing a judge.

And I am working up the nerve to tell Officer Hines just that, when he unlocks my cell and looks in on me and Ricky and points to me and says, "Visitor."

Down the long hall that is not all that different from the one that connects the science classrooms in my high school, I think of all the people it could be. My brother, here to kite me some smokes and tell me to keep my head up. My dad, to be less angry than he is just confused. My mom, to be angry at herself and me and probably to start a fight with a guard. Christine, to ask me where Eric is. The Man, to do whatever's left to do to me.

We round the corner and Officer Hines unlocks a little room and opens the door, and inside, sitting at a little table, is none of those people. It's a young, reasonably pretty, professional-looking woman. She gestures for me to sit down in a metal chair across the table from her.

"You okay?" Officer Hines asks.

"Yes," she says.

I sit down. Officer Hines leaves us alone.

"Hi," she says, less professionally than any lawyer I've ever seen on TV. "I'm here representing somebody who basically thought you'd know who they were without me having to identify them. Make sense?"

I think I know who she's talking about but I wonder why they switched from being represented by men in suits with black sunglasses to women who, absent the clothes and briefcase, seem like they should be selling cell-phone covers at the mall. I nod.

"Great. So . . . Yeesh. So . . . it is NOT very much fun in here. Right?"

I just stare at her.

"Right. Here's the thing. They told me not to say 'This can all go away.' BUT—" she says, and she smiles, and waves her hand like, "but there you have it." "You can be prosecuted for what you would stand accused of doing," she says, "or . . . you can *not* be prosecuted, be let go, and just, like . . . continue onward."

"Really?" I say.

She nods, once, not even a full nod. She just lowers her head in one sharp movement.

"Of course, contingent upon that . . . I mean, no-brainer . . . you don't say anything, to anyone, ever. It can all go away, it can all come back. Make sense?"

"Yes . . . You can do that?"

"I mean *I* can't do that. But you know, the people that I, you know, represent . . . they're very good."

We sit there for a second.

"Do you need some time to think about it?"

"Who do you work for?" I say.

She shrugs and smiles knowingly like, I don't know, I couldn't tell you if I did know, I am a recent college graduate employed by powers great and murderous and my name is Amy and I get to go home after this.

Two hours later my dad comes to pick me up and that's when he says the thing about he never thought I'd be the kid to end up in jail. In the passenger seat of his SUV the sky through the windshield seems particularly big and blue, but not in a pretty way. I think of rap lyrics I have heard my brother recite in the past about what happens to snitches who talk to buy their freedom, and I wonder if it is better or worse than what I deserve. Then I think, *I guess I didn't really snitch.* If anything I agreed NOT to talk. But then I think, *Wait, I did snitch.* I snitched to the guy from church when I was angry. Except *snitch* is the wrong word. Snitching is too cool. I told. I tattled like a little kid.

One kid, Eric Lederer, our high school, his dad's gun, "homemade weaponry," and doubtlessly evil plans foiled by our crack security staff and the local PD. That's the official story. He is now in federal custody, because some of the "homemade weaponry" may have strayed into domestic-terrorism territory.

My friend Eric has dirt all over his name, but mine is clean, at least in an official sense. According to my brother, the conventional wisdom at the school is that I had something to do with it, or failing that, that I knew enough to leave school that day before everything went down. I'm not there to hear it. I finish that year at a Catholic school where some of my brother's friends go, and I do my junior and senior years at another school on the north side of the city. Everywhere I go kids seem to have a vague understanding that I am not to be trusted. Someone tells me there is a Namespot group made by some kids at my old school called "DARREN BEN-NETT, HOW COME YOU GUYS WANTED TO KILL US?"

I could never rejoin the college kids at the house with the lemon tree from which Eric and I were going to conquer the world, because just about every kid who doesn't go out of state goes to that college and it would be the same kids who suspected I was ruined. I had to go across the country if I ever wanted to salvage anything of what we had that week or two where the world seemed like anything could happen in it. And my grades were okay and my record was clean, so I went.

"Homemade weaponry." That hurts the most. Like we never dreamed up a universe and made parts of it real and almost got away with it. Like Eric never meant that anything could exist. Like Eric never existed.

But of course, he did exist. That's why we have Symnitol now. I'm 90,000 percent sure they got him, they juiced his brain and precipitated it and all the other shit my lab partner used to gape at me in honors chemistry for not understanding, and now experts are debating whether it's a good or a bad thing that medically the human race no longer has to sleep. They are not going to be debating for long.

The world had something in its pure unadulterated form and I fucked up and now it's accessible to everybody, people who won't have the scruples to go out into the desert when the things they imagine start becoming real, people without the imagination to form things that deserve to become real, their thoughts will start appearing too, one-dimensional, all violence and fucked-upedness. The world as it isn't, it will be.

And it's a little bit of that stuff that's in me now, a little bit of Eric that has let me stay up all night writing this down without once feeling tired, and a messed-up thing is that the kid who could've told it way better than I could is gone. A kid who dreamed so hard it exploded from his head and into the world, promising everything. And I sold him out hard.

The only hope I have is that if I take enough of this stuff I will push myself to Eric's levels really fast, and if *TimeBlaze* was our story and he made it real, then this will be my story and all of the sudden it will be real and he will be back. He won't materialize; suddenly he will have been there all along. I will turn around and he will be standing there, a nerd standing over my desk, confident, not shifting from foot to foot, telling me my drawings are good. And I can tell him how sorry I am.

ACKNOWLEDGEMENTS

This book would not have been written if Eliza Skinner hadn't told me "you should write a novel" one day on the N train. Thanks are also due to my family, Dianne McGunigle, Greg Walter, Phil Cassese, Meggie McFadden and the rest of DERRICK, Daniel Greenberg, Gerry Howard, Tim O'Connell and everyone else at Vintage, Charlie Rubin, Emilie Spiegel, Steve Stout, Amy Eckman, WNBC, the UCB Theater, and anyone who read an early draft and gave me notes and encouragement. Also important were pop-punk music and the state of Arizona.